STRIPTEASE,
REPEAT PERFORMANCE,
and
THE PROPHETS

OTHER PLAYS BY SLAWOMIR MROZEK
PUBLISHED BY GROVE PRESS

The Elephant

Tango

Six Plays by Slawomir Mrozek
   The Martyrdom of Peter Ohey
   Enchanted Night
   The Police
   Out at Sea
   Charlie
   The Party

Vatzlav

STRIPTEASE,
REPEAT
PERFORMANCE,
and
THE
PROPHETS

Three Plays By
Slawomir Mrozek

Grove Press, Inc.   New York

CONTENTS

STRIPTEASE

Translated by Lola Gruenthal

Cast of Characters

MR. I
MR. II

The stage is bare except for two chairs. Two doors, one stage left and one stage right, should be in clear view of the audience. When the curtain rises there is no one on stage. One can hear strange rattling and rumbling noises which may sound vaguely familiar but cannot be identified. The door on stage left opens and MR. I *comes rushing in. He is middle-aged, neatly but conventionally dressed, and carries a briefcase. Obviously he is not interested in his present environment but is rather preoccupied with something that has just happened outside. He should convey the impression that he has not entered the stage of his own will. He finally looks around and adjusts his suit. The door remains slightly ajar. A few moments later* MR. II *rushes in through the door on stage right. He looks like an exact replica of* MR. I *and also carries a briefcase. The second door is not completely closed either.*

MR. I: Extraordinary!

MR. II: Incredible!

MR. I: I was walking along as usual . . .

MR. II: Not a care in the world . . .

MR. I: When suddenly . . .

MR. II: Like a bolt from the sky . . .

MR. I (*as though just becoming aware of the presence of* MR. II): How did you get here?

MR. II: Why don't you ask what brought me here, or who brought me here?

MR. I (*again following his own thoughts*): Outrageous!

MR. II (*as though slightly mimicking* MR. I): Preposterous!

MR. I: I was simply walking, or perhaps, rather, hurrying along . . .

MR. II: Yes, that's right! You were certainly heading for a particular destination.

MR. I: How do you know?

MR. II: It's obvious. I was walking along too, or rather, hurrying along, heading for my destination.

MR. I: You took the words right out of my mouth. As I said, I was heading for this destination when suddenly . . .

MR. II: And remember, this was a destination that you yourself had chosen.

MR. I: Exactly! And with conscious intent, mind you, with full conscious intent . . .

MR. II: Obeying the dictates of your conscience, motivated by faith and reason.

MR. I: You're reading my very thoughts. As I was saying, I followed the path most appropriate for my chosen destination when suddenly . . .

MR. II (*confidentially*): They beat you?

MR. I: Oh, no! (*Also confidentially.*) And you?

MR. II: God forbid! I mean, I don't know a thing. That's all I can say.

MR. I: What was it then?

MR. II: That's hard to say for sure. It was like a gigantic elephant blocking the street. Or were there riots? First I had the impression of a flood, then of a picnic. But being in such a fog . . .

MR. I: That's true! It's so foggy today you can hardly see a thing. Still, I was trying to reach my particular destination . . .

MR. II: Which you yourself had freely chosen . . .

MR. I: That's God's honest truth! Nothing was left to chance. I had prepared everything down to the last detail. My wife and I often spend long hours planning ahead, planning our entire lives.

MR. II: I also had it all mapped out in advance. Even as a child . . .

MR. I (*confidentially*): Did you hear a voice?

MR. II: I certainly did. There was a voice.

MR. I: Something like a saw . . . a persistent sound . . . no, actually an intermittent one.

MR. II: A gigantic buzz saw.

MR. I: But where the hell could a saw come from?

MR. II: Perhaps it wasn't a saw. Something threw me to the ground.

MR. I: But what?

MR. II: The worst part is this uncertainty. Was it really to the ground?

MR. I: Where else if not to the ground?

MR. II: But was I really thrown? What a jungle of riddles! I can't even tell if this was a "being-thrown" in the exact, classical sense, deserving of the name. Though I had the sensation of being thrown down, lying on the ground, I was perhaps——

MR. I (*tensely*): More overthrown than thrown down?

MR. II: Precisely! And to tell the truth, I really have no complaints. Did you see any people?

MR. I: Are there any at all?

MR. II: I suppose there are, but with all this fog . . . it doesn't seem likely.

MR. I: The worst of all is this lack of assurance.

MR. II: What color was it?

MR. I: What?

MR. II: It's so hard to figure out anything. It was something bright . . . a sort of rose color shot through with lead.

MR. I: Nonsense!

MR. II (*moving over to* MR. I, *after a pause*): And still they hit you in the jaw.

MR. I: Me?

MR. II: Me too.

Pause.

MR. I: Well, anyway, now I can't get there on time anymore.

MR. II: How about just walking out? Right now! As though nothing had happened?

MR. I: No, no!

MR. II: Are you afraid?

MR. I: Me? Why should I be? I'm just a little nervous. I just can't see . . .

MR. II: That's because of the fog.

MR. I: Did they say we must not leave the room?

MR. II: Who?

MR. I: Whom were you thinking of?

MR. II: Never mind!

MR. I: I've decided to stay put. The situation will clear up by itself.

MR. II: But why? It may be quite possible for us to leave this room, unimpeded, and to continue on our way. After all, we can't really tell what's going on. Perhaps we ourselves went astray.

MR. I: Are you blaming yourself? Us? We both knew where we were going, each of us heading for his specific destination.

MR. II: Then it was not our own fault?

MR. I: No, unless . . .

MR. II: Unless?

MR. I: How do I know? Let's drop the subject! I, for one, feel most strongly that we should not leave this room.

MR. II: If you're so sure about it . . .

MR. I: Definitely! We have to use sound reasoning in dealing with this matter.

Both sit down.

MR. II: Perhaps you're right. (*Listens.*) There's nobody there.

MR. I: Actually, there's no cause for concern, is there?

MR. II: No obvious cause, I would say.

MR. I: Are you implying that there is a cause . . . an obscure one?

MR. II: You have a mind of your own.

MR. I: Let's establish the facts.

MR. II: All right, go ahead.

MR. I: Very well, then: Each of us left his house according to plan and walked, or rather hurried, as you observed correctly, in the direction of his goal. The morning was brisk, the weather fair, the existence of wife and children an established fact. Each of us knew whatever there was to be known. Of course, we had no exact idea about the kind of molecules, not to speak of atoms, that our bedside tables are composed of, but, after all, there are specialists who deal with such matters. Basically, everything was perfectly clear. Wellshaved, carrying our practical and indispensable briefcases, we set out purposefully toward our goal. The respective addresses had been thoroughly committed to memory. But to be quite safe we had also noted them down in our notebooks. Am I correct?

MR. II: On every point.

MR. I: Now listen carefully! At a certain moment, as we were pursuing our course, a course that we had mapped out in detail and that was, so to speak, the end result of all our rational calculations, something happened which . . . and this is a point I must stress . . . came entirely from the outside, something separate in itself and independent of us.

MR. II: With regard to this point, I must register some doubt. Since we are unable to define the exact nature of the occurrence, and since we cannot even agree as to its manifestations . . . due to the fog or to whatever other causes . . . we are in no position to state with any degree of certainty that this something came exclusively from the outside or that it was entirely separate in itself and independent of us.

MR. I: You are discomposing me.

MR. II: I beg your pardon?

MR. I: You're interrupting my thoughts.

MR. II: I'm sorry.

MR. I: Unfortunately, we are not able to determine the exact nature of the phenomenon, and . . .

MR. II: That's just what I said.

MR. I: If you wish to go on, don't mind me!

MR. II: The words just slipped out. It won't happen again.

MR. I (*continuing*): We cannot even determine with any appropriate degree of accuracy what particular elements constituted this something. (*Pause.*) I beg your pardon?

MR. II: I didn't say a thing.

MR. I: I, for instance, perceived something that seemed to have the shape of an animal, but still I cannot be absolutely sure that it was not at the same time a mineral. Actually, it seems to me that it involved energy rather than matter. I think all this may be best defined as a phenomenon hovering on the borderline of dimensions and definitions, a connecting link between color, form, smell, weight, length, and breadth, shade, light, dark, and so on and so forth.

MR. II: Do you still feel any pain? Mine is almost all gone.

MR. I: Please don't reduce everything to its lowest level!

MR. II: I was just asking.

MR. I (*continuing his train of thought*): This much is certain: We were helpless in the face of the phenomenon, and, partly of our own will, as we were looking for shelter, partly due to external pressure, we happened to find ourselves in these strange quarters which at that critical moment were close at hand. Fortunately, we found the doors open. Needless to say, our original intentions have thus been completely upset and, as it were, arrested.

MR. II: I fully agree. What are your conclusions?

MR. I: This is just what I was coming to. Our main task now is to preserve our calm and our personal dignity. Thus, it would seem to me, we still remain in control of the situation. Basically, our freedom is in no way limited.

MR. II: You call this freedom, our sitting here?

MR. I: But we can walk out at any moment . . . the doors are open.

MR. II: Then let's go! We've wasted too much time anyway.

Again the same strange noise is heard as in the beginning.

MR. I: What . . . ? What's that?

MR. II: I told you we should go.

MR. I: Right now?

MR. II: Are you afraid?

MR. I: Not at all.

MR. II: First you insist on preserving your personal dignity by asserting your freedom, and then you don't even want to leave while there is still time.

MR. I: If I left right now I would limit the idea of freedom.

MR. II: What do you mean?

MR. I: It's quite obvious. What is freedom? It is the capacity of making a choice. As long as I am sitting here, knowing that I can walk out of this door, I am free. But as soon as I get up and walk out, I have already made my choice, I have limited the possible courses of action, I have lost my freedom. I become the slave of my own locomotion.

MR. II: But your sitting here and not walking out is just another way of making a choice. You simply choose sitting rather than leaving.

MR. I: Wrong! While I'm sitting, I can still leave. If, however, I do leave, I preclude the alternative of sitting.

MR. II: And this makes you feel comfortable?

MR. I: Perfectly comfortable. Unlimited inner freedom, that is my answer to these strange happenings. (MR. II *gets up.*) What are you doing?

MR. II: I'm leaving. I don't like this.

MR. I: Are you joking?

MR. II: I'm not trying to. I believe in external freedom.

MR. I: And what about me?

MR. II: Goodbye.

MR. I: Please wait! Are you crazy? You don't even know what's out there!

Both doors close slowly.

MR. II: Hey! What's going on now?

MR. I: Don't close them! Don't close them!

MR. II: All because of your babbling! We should have made up our minds right away.

MR. I: You don't have to blame me. If you had sat still, the doors wouldn't have closed. It was your fault.

MR. II: Now there's no way of finding out.

MR. I: It's all because of you. Thanks to your behavior we've lost our chance to get out.

MR. II *goes to one of the doors and tries unsuccessfully to open it.*

MR. II: Hey! Open up right now!

MR. I: Shh! Be quiet!

MR. II: Why should I be quiet?

MR. I: I don't know.

MR. II (*goes to the other door, knocks, and listens*): Locked!

MR. I: Do me a favor and sit down!

MR. II: Well, where is it now, your precious freedom?

MR. I: I have nothing to blame myself for. My freedom remains unaffected.

MR. II: But there's no way to get out now, is there?

MR. I: The potential of my freedom has remained unchanged. I have not made a choice, I have in no way confined myself. The doors were closed for external reasons. I am the same person that I was before. As you may have noticed, I did not even get up from my chair.

MR. II: These doors are upsetting me.

MR. I: My dear sir, while we are unable to influence external events, we must make every effort to preserve our dignity and our inner balance. And with regard to those, we command an unlimited field, even though the infinite variety of choices has been reduced to two alternatives. These, of course, exist only as long as we do not choose either of them.

MR. II: What else could happen?

MR. I: Do you think it may get worse?

MR. II: I'll try to knock on the wall . . . perhaps somebody is there.

MR. I: It is regrettable that you have no regard for the inviolable nature of your personal freedom. I, too, could knock on the wall, but I won't. If I did, I would preclude other possibilities, such as reading the papers I have in my briefcase or concentrating on last year's horse races.

MR. II *knocks on the wall several times and listens; he repeats this for a while. Then he takes off one shoe and bangs with it against the wall. One of the doors opens slowly, and in comes a Hand of supernatural size. It resembles the old-fashioned printer's symbol: Hand with pointing index finger and attached cuff. The palm should be brightly colored to make it stand out clearly against the scenery. With bent index finger the Hand makes a monotonously repeated gesture in the direction of* MR. II, *beckoning to him.*

MR. I (*the first to notice the Hand*): Pssst! (MR. II *has not yet seen the Hand; he keeps banging with his shoe and listening.*) Pssst! Stop it, please! Don't you see what's going on?

MR. II *turns around.* MR. I *points to the Hand.*

MR. II: Something new again!

The Hand continues beckoning to him. MR. II *walks over to it. The Hand points to the shoe he is holding, then it reaches out in an ambiguous gesture that may be either begging or demanding. Hesitantly,* MR. II *puts his shoe into the Hand. The Hand disappears and returns immediately without the shoe.* MR. II *takes off*

*his other shoe and gives it to the Hand. The Hand
leaves the room, returns, and repeatedly touches* MR. II's
*stomach with its index finger. Guessing what this
means,* MR. II *takes off his belt and hands it over. The
Hand withdraws, returns without the belt, and begins
to beckon to* MR. I.

MR. I: Me? (*He slowly walks over to the Hand, stopping at
every other step. While he is talking, the Hand con-
tinually beckons to him.*) But I didn't knock . . . There
must be a misunderstanding . . . I didn't make a choice
. . . no choice whatsoever . . . I did not knock, though
I must admit that when my colleague knocked I was
hoping that someone might hear it and come in, that
the situation might be cleared up and that we would
be allowed to leave. This much I admit, but I didn't
do any knocking. (*The Hand points to his shoes.*)
I protest. I repeat once more: The knocking was not
done by me. I don't understand why I should hand
over my shoes. (*Bends down to untie the laces.*) I
value my inner freedom. A little patience, please!
Can't the Hand see that there's a knot here? . . . Personally, I don't hold anything against the Hand, because my own conscience is clear. I am determined to
save my inner freedom, even at the cost of my external
freedom . . . quite the opposite to my colleague here.
But I'm not holding anything against him either, because, after all, what he does is his own business. I re-
quest only that we be treated as individuals, each
according to his own views . . . Just a moment, I'm get-

ting it. There's no fire, is there? (*Giving the Hand his shoes.*) Glad to oblige! (*The Hand points to his stomach.*) I'm not wearing a belt ... I prefer suspenders. All right, I'll give up the suspenders, too, if necessary. (*Takes off his jacket and unbuttons his suspenders.*) Peculiar methods they have here! All right, here they are ... Somebody's fingernails could use a good cleaning, if I may venture an opinion. (*The Hand disappears, the door closes slowly.*) At least I'm wearing a fresh pair of socks. I'm glad about that.

MR. II: Boot licker!

MR. I: Leave me alone! I'm not bothering you.

MR. II: What can I use now to knock with?

MR. I: That's your problem. I'm going to sit down. (*Returns to his chair.*)

MR. II: You're in good shape now with your inner freedom. You're losing your pants.

MR. I: What about yours? They won't stay up either without a belt.

MR. II: Well, what do you make of all this?

MR. I: I can only repeat what I said before: First the dear Hand interfered with my free movement in space and then with my ability to wear trousers. This is true, and this I'm willing to admit. But what does it matter? All these are externals. Inwardly I have remained free. I have not become engaged in any action, I have not made any gesture. I haven't even moved a finger. Just sitting here I am still free to do whatever lies in the realm of possibility. Not you, though. You did something . . . you made a choice . . . you knocked against the wall and made a fool of yourself. Slave!

MR. II: I could slap your face, but there are more important things to be done.

MR. I: Right. But why do they deal with us like this?

MR. II: It's always the first thing they do . . . take away your shoe laces, belts, and suspenders.

MR. I: What for?

MR. II: So you can't hang yourself.

MR. I: You must be joking! If I'm not even getting up from my chair, how can I hang myself? Of course, I could if I wanted to, but I won't. You know my views.

MR. II: I'm sick and tired of your views.

MR. I: That's your problem. But listen to this: If the dear Hand doesn't want us to hang ourselves, this means that it wants to keep us alive. That's a good sign!

MR. II: This is just what bothers me. It means that the Hand thinks of us in terms of categories . . . Life and the other . . . what's it called?

MR. I: Death?

MR. II: You said it.

Pause.

MR. I: I am calm.

MR. II: Tell me, what could you do now, if you felt like doing something? Of course, taking into account the fact that you had to relinquish your shoes and suspenders.

MR. I: Oh, quite a few things. I could, for instance, put on my jacket inside out, roll up the legs of my trousers, and pretend to be a fisherman.

MR. II: And what else?

MR. I: I could sing.

MR. II: That's enough. (*Turns up the legs of his trousers, puts on his jacket inside out, and takes off his socks.*)

MR. I: Are you crazy? What are you trying to do?

MR. II: I'm pretending to be a fisherman, and I'm going to sing, too. In contrast to you, I want to explore all the possibilities of action. Maybe the Hand is partial to fishermen and lets them return to freedom. Who knows? One should not neglect any possibility. I've asked you because you have more imagination than I. For instance, I could never have thought up all those things about inner freedom.

MR. I: It's all right with me. But please remember that I'm not moving from this chair.

MR. II: You don't have to. (*He climbs on the chair and sings Schubert's "The Trout." One of the doors slowly opens.*)

MR. I (*who has been anxiously watching the door*): Now you've done it!

The Hand appears.

MR. II: How do you know? Perhaps I'll be allowed to go and you'll keep sitting. (*The Hand beckons to him.*) I'm coming, I'm coming. What's it all about? (*The Hand indicates that it wants his jacket.*) But I was just—— Is there a law against fishing? (*The Hand repeats its gesture.*) I was just pretending. I'm not really a fisherman. (*Gives the Hand his jacket. The Hand disappears, comes back, and now obviously requests his trousers.*) No, I won't give up the trousers! (*The Hand forms a fist and slowly rises.*) All right. (*He takes off his trousers.*)

MR. I (*getting up*): Me too?

After waiting for an answer, which he does not receive, MR. I voluntarily removes his jacket. Meanwhile MR. II has given the Hand his trousers, and he now stands there in striped knee-length underpants. The Hand carries the trousers backstage, returns immediately and beckons to MR. I.

MR. I: All right, here it is. I'm not resisting, and I beg the Hand to take this into consideration. (*He gives his jacket to the Hand, which takes it out and returns immediately.*) I'm always willing to oblige ... may I keep my trousers in return? (*The Hand makes a negative gesture.*) All right, I won't protest.

He takes off his trousers and stands up in his underpants, identical to those of MR. II. The Hand disappears, the door closes.

MR. I: You can go to hell with your idea about fishermen.
MR. II: It seems to me that it was your idea.
MR. I: But you carried it out. It's cold in here.
MR. II: It's quite possible that we might have been ordered to hand over our clothes anyway, idea or no idea.
MR. I: No! I'm convinced it was you who got us both into this predicament with your idiotic masquerade. It was you who attracted the Hand's attention to our clothing. If at least you had not rolled up your trousers, they would not have caught its eye.

MR. II: But fishermen always roll up their trousers.

MR. I: What good does that do you now?

MR. II: You can't keep ignoring the fact that we differ in our views. You do nothing so that you can feel free to do anything—of course, within the range of what is permitted—while I try to do everything I am permitted to do. But apparently wearing trousers is not permitted.

MR. I: You yourself have brought this down on your head.

MR. II: An anatomical inaccuracy! Besides, let me repeat this once more: We don't know whether the removal of our clothes was provoked by my action or whether it was part of a predetermined plan.

MR. I: At least now you should realize that my basic attitude is superior to yours. Don't you see: I didn't knock, I didn't sing, I didn't roll up my trousers, and still, here I am, looking just like you. Even our stripes are the same.

MR. II: Where is your superiority then?

MR. I: No waste of energy; same results. Plus, of course, my sense of inner freedom which . . .

MR. II: One more word about inner freedom and that will be the end of you.

MR. I (*backing up*): You're unfair! After all, everyone has a right to choose the philosophy that suits him best.

MR. II: Never mind! I can't stand this anymore!

MR. I: I'm warning you: I won't defend myself. Defending oneself involves making a choice, and for me this is out, in the name of . . .

MR. II: What? Go on! In the name of what?

MR. I (*hesitantly*): In the name of inner free—— (MR. II

throws himself at him. MR. I *runs all over the stage.*)
Keep your hands off!

*The door opens and the Hand reappears, beckoning to
both.* MR. I *and* MR. II *come to a sudden halt.*

MR. II: Me?
MR. I: Or me?
MR. II: Maybe it's you . . .
MR. I: You started this fight. Now you'll get your just de-
serts.
MR. II: Why me? Do you still believe that your idiotic
theory is better?
MR. I: And you believe that your vulgar pragmatism, this
lack of any theory, will stand up to such a test?

The Hand beckons to both.

MR. II: We'd better go over! It wants something again.
MR. I: All right, let's go! We'll soon find out who is right.

*They go over to the Hand which links them together
with a pair of handcuffs. The Hand disappears and the
door closes.* MR. II *drags* MR. I *along with him by the
chain of the handcuffs and collapses on his chair.
Silence.*

MR. I: What does this mean? (*Anxiously.*) Aren't you feel-
ing well? Do you believe that this time it's serious?
Say something, please!
MR. II: I'm afraid . . .
MR. I: Of what?
MR. II: So far the Hand has limited only our freedom of
movement in space. But what assurance is there that

soon we won't be limited in something even more essential?

MR. I: In what?

MR. II: In time. In our own duration.

Pause.

MR. I: I don't know either. (*Pedantically.*) You, of course, being an activist, will exhaust your energies more rapidly. I, on the other hand, conserve mine . . .

MR. II (*imploringly*): Not again!

MR. I: I'm sorry. I didn't mean to hurt your feelings. Do you have a plan?

MR. II: There is only one thing we can do now.

MR. I: What?

MR. II: Apologize to the Hand.

MR. I: Apologize? But what for? We haven't done anything to the Hand. On the contrary, it should . . .

MR. II: This is completely irrelevant. We have to apologize all the same . . . in general, for no reason. To save ourselves . . . for whatever good it may do.

MR. I: No, I can't do that. I don't suppose I have to explain my reasons.

MR. II: You're right, I know them by heart. To apologize to the Hand would mean to make a choice, which again would limit your freedom, and so on and so forth.

MR. I: Yes, that's how it is.

MR. II: Do as you please! In any case, I am going to apologize. One has to abase oneself. Perhaps that is what it expects us to do.

MR. I: I would like to join you, but my principles . . .

24 / Slawomir Mrozek

MR. II: I have nothing more to say.

MR. I: I think I can see a way out. You're going to force me to apologize with you. In that case there is no question of choice on my part. I'm simply going to be forced.

MR. II: All right, consider yourself forced.

The door opens.

MR. I: I think it's coming. (*The Hand appears.*) If only we had some flowers! (*Whispering.*) You start!

Both run over to the Hand. MR. II *clears his throat in preparation for his apology.*

MR. II: Dear Hand! I mean, Dear and Most Honorable Hand! Although well aware of the fact that the Hand is not here to listen to us, we still beg permission to speak to the Hand from the heart . . . I mean, we would like to hand the Hand a confession, although somewhat belated, nevertheless with full conscious awareness, we sincerely beg to apologize for . . . for . . . (*Whispering to* MR. I.) For what?

MR. I: For walking, for going ahead, for everything in general . . .

MR. II: For walking, for going ahead, for . . . I'm expressing myself poorly, but I simply wish to apologize in general . . . for having been . . . for being . . . begging forgiveness from the depth of my heart for whatever the Honorable Hand knows that we don't know . . . for how are we to know what there is to be known? Therefore, whatever the case may be, I humbly apologize, I beg the Hand's forgiveness, I kiss the Hand. (*He ceremoniously kisses the Hand.*)

MR. I: I wish to join my colleague, though only in a certain sense, having been forced ... The Hand knows my principles ... Therefore, though being forced, I nevertheless sincerely apologize to the Hand on principle.

He ceremoniously kisses the Hand. Meanwhile the other door opens and through it appears a Second Hand, completely covered by a red glove. It beckons to both. MR. II *notices it first. Both turn their backs to the First Hand.*

MR. II: There! Look!

MR. I: Another one!

MR. II: There are always two.

MR. I: It's calling us.

MR. II: Should we go? (*The First Hand covers his head with a conical cardboard hood.*) I can't see anything!

MR. I: It's calling us. (*The First Hand covers his head with an identical hood.*) It's dark.

MR. II: When you're called, you have to go.

Handcuffed to each other and blinded by the hoods, they move toward stage center. Constantly stumbling and swerving, they gradually come closer to the Second Hand.

MR. I: The briefcases! We forgot our briefcases!

MR. II: Right! My briefcase! Where's my briefcase?

They grope blindly for their briefcases, left standing next to the chairs, then pick them up and follow the Second Hand through the door. Blackout.

REPEAT PERFORMANCE

A Play in Two Acts

Translated by Teresa Dzieduszycka
and Ralph Manheim

Cast of Characters

DADDY
SHE
THE GHOST
THE LITTLE FELLOW

ACT I

A large room. At the rear, two windows placed symmetri-
cally. Behind the windows slightly faded trees against a
background of blue sky. Green shutters opening inward.
Between the windows a gilded frame in which there was
once a picture. Nearer the proscenium stage right, a round
table covered by a green cloth. Over the table hangs an oil
lamp with a large porcelain shade. Several wicker arm-
chairs. Identical doors in the right and left walls. On each
of these walls, exactly centered, a pair of stag's antlers.

Through the door on the stage right enter SHE and DADDY.
SHE is a pretty girl of eighteen wearing a sleeveless violet
minidress, white stockings, and black, low-heeled, patent-
leather shoes. She has a carry-all and a small pocketbook.

DADDY is a man just under fifty, large and powerful. A
massive face, bristling with health though slightly apoplectic. Close-shaved except for a clipped pepper-and-salt moustache. Conservative dark suit with vest, of an old-fashioned
cut. Bow-tie. Bowler hat. He is carrying a suitcase and an
umbrella. He sets the suitcase in the corner to stage right of
the entrance, between the stage right wall and the rear
wall. He takes her carry-all and puts it down beside his suitcase. He keeps his umbrella in his hand.

SHE (looking around): Where are we?
DADDY: Guess.

SHE: I don't have to. (SHE *sinks down dramatically on the sofa.*) I'm ruined.

DADDY: Ruined?

SHE: You've compromised me.

DADDY: Compromised you?

SHE: You're despicable, despicable.

DADDY: What *is* the matter with you?

SHE: This is a hotel.

DADDY: Certainly not.

SHE (*suddenly matter-of-fact*): Then what is it?

DADDY: How shall I put it . . .

SHE (*again tragic*): Don't deny it! I knew, I knew it would end like this. Some provincial hotel. The bellboys with their knowing smiles. And naturally you've only taken one room. Oh, it's all so sordid. . . . (SHE *weeps, sniffling and trying to make the tears flow.*)

DADDY: You're mistaken.

SHE: At least have the courage to admit it. You abominable egotist, you're ruining my life. You haven't kept your word.

DADDY: But——

SHE: And you deny it! They'll know all about me, and they'll tell . . . you know who.

SHE *sobs rather exaggeratedly.*

DADDY: Calm yourself, I beg you. This is not a hotel.

SHE: Of course not. It's worse! It's some filthy stinking roadhouse! Not even a bed, not even a closet or a telephone . . . (SHE *interrupts herself, takes a mirror out of*

her handbag, and looks at herself.) Good God, look
at me!

DADDY (*glad to change the subject*): Adorable.

SHE: Horrible. Ring for the chambermaid. (*Opens her suitcase, rummages through it.*) What are you waiting
for? I need an iron.

DADDY: If you'd only listen——

SHE: I'll ring myself. Where's the bell?

DADDY: In the first place, if I ring, someone will come in
and see you in my compromising company.

SHE: That's right. I forgot.

DADDY: In the second place, if someone comes in, he'll see
me in your compromising company.

SHE: No, don't ring!

DADDY: In the third place, I won't ring because there's no
bell. In the fourth place, even if I did ring, no one
would come because nobody else is here.

SHE: What do you mean, nobody?

DADDY: Not a living soul.

SHE: Then this isn't a hotel?

DADDY: That's what I've been trying to tell you. (*He hangs
his umbrella on the back of a chair, takes her by the
hand, and leads her to the window, stage right. He
opens the window wide.*) What do you see?

SHE: Trees. Woods.

DADDY: A forest. An old forest. There's no one here but us.

SHE: Then you've lied to me.

DADDY: I've . . . ?

SHE: Yes. You promised me a surprise.

DADDY: Isn't this a surprise?

SHE: Certainly not. When somebody promises me a surprise, it means a beautiful hotel in some beautiful resort. On the seashore, or in the mountains. And where have you brought me? To some dump.

DADDY: Let's not exaggerate. It's very nice here.

SHE: I thought I deserved a little luxury. Can't you afford it?

DADDY (*irritated*): But ... if that's what you wanted, it wouldn't have been a surprise.... Hotels! ... Resorts! ... Rubbish!

SHE: Wrong! I'd have been surprised to see a man keep his word.

DADDY *slaps her face.*

DADDY: And now go stand in the corner! (*Sobbing like a child,* SHE *goes to the corner.*) On your knees!

SHE: I don't want to.

DADDY: On your knees, I say! (SHE *kneels with her back to the audience.*) Did you really think you could take that tone with me?

SHE: Why did you hit me?

DADDY: Tantrums, scenes, hysterics, reproaches ... What is the meaning of this? Do you take me for your lover?

SHE: But——

DADDY: That will do!

SHE: But——

DADDY: You forget who I am.

SHE: But you——

DADDY: Stop it!

SHE: But you've got to be my lover.

Pause.

DADDY: What makes you think that?

SHE: You told me so yourself.

DADDY: Nothing of the sort.

SHE: You implied it.

DADDY: How dare you suspect me of such a thing!

SHE: You said you liked me.

DADDY: And you had the impudence to believe me! (*Pause.*) Even if it were true. First of all, remember you owe me your respect. I can say what I like, it's your duty to be modest and behave yourself.

SHE: Yes, Daddy.

DADDY (*again losing his temper*): And not to exasperate me.

SHE: I won't do it again.

DADDY: Or torture me!

SHE: No, never again.

DADDY (*lowering his voice*): Why not?

SHE: Because you don't want me to.

DADDY: But suppose I do want you to?

SHE (*still kneeling, turns toward the audience, hopefully*): Then we're going to do something wicked?

DADDY: If I don't change my mind.

SHE: Too bad! (SHE *sits down on the floor.*) You disappoint me.

DADDY: I haven't changed my mind yet.

SHE: But you haven't the same charm anymore.

DADDY (*disconcerted*): You don't like me?

SHE: Not as much as before. You were wonderful before.

DADDY: And not now?

SHE: You're getting tedious. Do this, do that, this is allowed, this isn't . . . Now I'm sorry I came!

DADDY: I'm obliged to be severe. Discipline is indispensable.

SHE: Exactly. You were different before. More diabolical.

DADDY: I'm still diabolical!

SHE: Indecent, disconcerting. You gave me the cold chills.

DADDY (*alarmed*): And now you've recovered?

SHE: You surprised me. It was beautiful. First you were a plain ordinary daddy. In slippers and dressing gown, just like any other . . . uninteresting. And then suddenly a seducer, an entirely different man. And the best part . . .

Pause.

DADDY: Go on.

SHE: You won't scold?

DADDY: I permit you to speak.

SHE: Still a daddy, but different. So magnificently incestuous.

DADDY: What!

SHE: I'm sorry.

DADDY: My child, the word is inapplicable.

SHE: Then it's not incest?

DADDY: In the exact sense of the word—no.

SHE: But it's a sin, isn't it?

DADDY: While we're on the subject, permit me to point out that incest—or whatever you choose to call it—occurs even in the Bible. In the Old Testament, for instance. Even in the most pious families.

SHE (*springs up and cries out*): You've always got to spoil everything!

DADDY: I assure you that even today such cases are extremely frequent. On the sly, of course, so no one ever finds out.

SHE: And now you tell me it's nothing at all, and you make me get down on my knees because you want everything to be like at school. And I thought we were going to do something awful.

DADDY: Don't exaggerate.

SHE (*with enthusiasm*): Something . . . horrible.

DADDY: Childish illusions.

SHE: Something appalling!

DADDY: That isn't nice.

SHE: Something really monstrous!

DADDY: That's depraved!

SHE: I want to perpetrate something.

DADDY: But exactly what?

SHE: Something that isn't done.

DADDY (*shouting*): I forbid you to talk like that! (*Pause.*) Why?

SHE: For spite.

DADDY: Against whom?

SHE: All of you.

DADDY: For instance?

SHE: The whole world.

DADDY: Including me?

SHE: Everybody.

DADDY: But why do you want to be spiteful?

SHE: You can't understand. You're too grown up.

DADDY: Fortunately.

SHE: He'd understand.

DADDY: Who?

SHE: My husband.

Pause.

DADDY: Good. Let's drink to his health. (*Takes a bottle of cognac and two silver glasses from his suitcase. He pours the cognac, gives her a glass, then snaps to attention and ceremoniously raises his own.*) To the bridegroom's health!

SHE: Why so solemn? This isn't the wedding.

DADDY: I wasn't invited.

SHE: Anyway, I don't care for ceremonies.

DADDY (*obstinately*): To the bridegroom's health.

SHE (*setting her glass down on the table*): I don't want to.

DADDY: Drink. I like the old traditions.

SHE: I don't feel like it.

DADDY: Don't you wish him well?

SHE: Yes, but you're mean.

DADDY: No, I'm not. When I say "To the bridegroom's health," I mean it sincerely. I've never had a chance to drink to his health . . . with you. That's all.

SHE: Why do you persecute him? What has he done to you?

DADDY: Drink first. Then I'll tell you. (SHE *takes her glass. They drink a toast.* DADDY *puts his glass down on the table and kisses her on the forehead.*) I welcome you to my house.

SHE (*repulsing him*): You know, you're behaving like a pig.

DADDY: Watch your tongue.

SHE: It's disgusting to treat the poor boy like this.

DADDY: It's none of your business.

SHE: It's no way to behave.

DADDY: And that's no way to talk to your elders.

SHE: You scold me, you say I'm depraved, but you shouldn't do what you're doing.

DADDY: What am I doing?

SHE: Wronging him.

DADDY: That will do!

Pause. SHE *puts her glass on the table.*

SHE: Do you want me to tell you?

DADDY: What?

SHE: Who my husband is . . .

DADDY: No need to.

SHE: Just in case you'd forgotten.

DADDY: That'll do, I said!

SHE: Because maybe you've forgotten . . .

DADDY (*calmly*): All right. Then *I'll* tell *you*. Is that what you want? I know your husband better than you do. Yes, I know him well. I've known him for seventeen years. Do you want me to tell you who he is? A young whippersnapper who doesn't even know how to be married.

SHE: I don't agree with you.

DADDY: Don't interrupt. I'll do the talking. A young snot-nose without character, energy, or talent. Without me he'd have gone to the dogs long ago. Moreover, if it weren't for me, he wouldn't even be in this world.

Wrong him! How can I wrong him when he owes me everything? I gave him everything he has. Even his life!

SHE: He didn't ask you for it.

DADDY: But he took it. What do you know about him, what can you know about him? Whom have you known? Someone who says "I"; who says "I am," "I was," "I will be," "I wish." As if he had a right to. No, I'm the only one who really knows him. I saw him when he crawled on the ground, when he was afraid of the dark. When he chortled like an imbecile because somebody showed him two crossed fingers. Later, I only had to raise my voice to make him tremble and go pale with fright. I watched him approach me, humble, clumsy, hesitant, eager for anything and capable of nothing. When he thought I wasn't looking, I saw him gaping into the void, searching in stupid befuddlement for some way to win the affection of the world. (*Imitating him.*) "How should . . ." He wanted to be admitted, accepted, forgiven. And later I knew him as a school-boy, a dunce, and a clown. His pitiful attempts to seem strong and capable, to seem to be somebody! Impostor! Fraud! I knew his misery, his hidden tears, his revolting secrets. So I know what I'm saying. He's not even a man. He's barely my son.

SHE: You're being unfair.

DADDY (*sits down in the chair, tired by his harangue*): Really? What makes you think so?

SHE: For instance . . . (*Pause.*) He has a good heart, for instance.

DADDY (*contemptuously*): He's soft.

SHE: He's sweet.

DADDY: Out of cowardice.

SHE: Handsome.

DADDY: He gets that from his father. But nothing else.

SHE: Young . . .

DADDY: What!

SHE (*with emphasis*): Young.

Pause.

DADDY: That will pass.

SHE: He loves me.

DADDY: Oh, so that's it? Did he tell you so?

SHE: Yes.

DADDY: And as a proof of his love, he married you. Is that right?

SHE: Of course.

DADDY: In other words, he deceived you.

SHE: Please . . .

DADDY: Naturally you prefer to believe that he married you for yourself. The truth is that he married you entirely on my account. To prove to me that he's finally grown up. To show me that he's somebody. To impress me. A last, desperate, hopeless, stupid try. Like everything he tries to do. I'll never forget the moment when he came to me with the news. "I'm married, Daddy," he said, and he looked at me as if to say: "Now I'm your equal. Now we're even. I'm not a son anymore. I'm a husband." He was almost triumphant. He was insolent.

SHE: And what did you say?

DADDY (*standing up*): I took up the challenge.

SHE: That's no reason for persecuting him.

DADDY: He offended me.

SHE: How? By marrying me?

DADDY: Yes.

SHE: Me in particular?

DADDY: You've guessed it.

SHE: You don't like me?

DADDY: On the contrary.

SHE: Oh, so that's it.

DADDY: That was the basis of his infamous plan. Knowing that I would desire you, he brought you into my home. He wanted to look on while I gazed at you like an old beggar who hasn't even the right to beg. You were to be his revenge on me. I was to suffer without hope, in secret, but under his eyes. Oh no, he had no qualms about me . . . or you, either. I remember every single time he left your bedroom door ajar or let you run around the house half naked. Morning after morning he looked at me at the breakfast table with that stupid, arrogant smile on his pimply face, while you, still half asleep, were sitting between the two of us. Just seeing you in the street, even a fleeting glance, would have been enough to destroy my peace of mind. But he brought you into my home, forced me to live in your presence, near you and yet so far. Without a moment's respite.

SHE: Did it really upset you so much?

DADDY: That's why I say he offended me.

SHE: I knew you had something on your mind, but I didn't know it was me.

DADDY: Hypocrite!

SHE: You take it too much to heart.

DADDY: Too much to heart! The sleepless nights I've spent! On your account! But that's not the worst. The worst part was that he knew it and that that's what he wanted. I swear to you that more than once I wanted to throw you both out. But that would have crowned his triumph. He wanted me to suffer in silence or frankly surrender. Wait and see, I said to myself, you'll get results all right, but they won't be what you expected. Because he had offended me doubly.

SHE: What else did the poor boy do to you?

DADDY: Something much worse. He didn't take me seriously.

SHE: What does that mean?

DADDY: He wasn't afraid of me.

SHE: What was there to be afraid of?

DADDY: Me, of course. He thought he could persecute me with impunity. A father-in-law! Good joke! He thought being a father-in-law was a chain that would hold me like an old dog! That he wouldn't have to be jealous of me, to fear me anymore. That I was too old to be a threat to him. He offended me by not being afraid of me. That is why I decided to make you my mistress.

SHE: Well, I'll be damned! (*With a sigh.*) Poor little fellow . . . (*Pause.*) Then it's definite?

DADDY: Absolutely.

SHE: And if I'm not willing?

DADDY: I'll seduce you.

SHE: Now?

DADDY: Or, rather, I'll permit you to become my mistress. Only remember, no impudence . . .

SHE: So you permit me . . .

DADDY: Yes. But only on condition that you behave properly.

SHE: A prize for good deportment.

DADDY: I will tolerate no misbehavior.

SHE: So if I'm very good Daddy will permit me to profane the sacred bonds of matrimony . . .

DADDY: Only if you've deserved it. (SHE *takes her carry-all from the corner and throws her things into it.*) Where are you——

SHE: I'm going home.

DADDY: You mean you don't want to be unfaithful to him?

SHE: Certainly not.

DADDY: But I permit you to.

SHE: Who cares?

DADDY: I'll go further: I authorize you to.

SHE: Not enough.

DADDY: I command you to!

SHE: Don't make me laugh.

DADDY: What did you say? (*Pause.*) I see. You're joking. (SHE *picks up her carry-all. He takes it away from her and puts it back on the floor.*) You're not going anywhere.

SHE (*indignantly*): Oooh!

DADDY: Let's forget about these family matters. Never mind the little fellow. Very well. I won't give myself to you

as a father-in-law. Not even as a public figure, charged
with responsibilities, esteemed by society. What does
all that amount to? No! I will be the passion of your
life. An element, a force of nature!

SHE: You?

DADDY: Consider me simply as a Greek god.

SHE: You?

DADDY: Exactly. Come closer. (*In an undertone.*) I'm going
to tell you something.

SHE (*approaching*): I'm listening, Daddy.

DADDY: I'm not Daddy. I'm Zeus.

SHE: What?

DADDY: Like Zeus, I meant. The one in mythology. A
kind of metaphor to bring out my meaning... You
must have learned about him in school. Didn't they
teach you that?

SHE: I think I've heard the name.

DADDY: Well, that's who I am. Daddy is only one of my in-
carnations. To hell with Daddy! The essential is the
force that is in me. Daddy is only a symbol, like a
whirlwind, storm, or lightning—the visible signs of his
power. Look at me. (*He removes his hat, revealing his
bald head.*) You see the frost on my temples? That's
exactly what I wanted to tell you: I'm not a youngster.

SHE: So what?

DADDY: Where do you find the eternal snows? Only on the
summits. The green grass grows in the plains, it fades
in the autumn. You will attain to the summits. I am
Kilimanjaro.

SHE: What?

DADDY (*hesitantly*): Kilimanjaro . . .

SHE: Nonsense. (*Picks up her carry-all and goes to stage right.*)

DADDY: Don't go.

SHE: Why not?

DADDY: Because I'm asking you.

SHE: Oh, that's different. (*Comes back.*) But I want to know why you're asking me.

DADDY: Not exactly asking. No . . . I'm urging you. That's it. Urging you! (SHE *returns to stage right.*) Don't go!

SHE (*returning*): All right. I'll stay. But only on one condition.

DADDY (*without assurance*): What condition . . . ?

SHE: That you get down on your knees . . .

DADDY: Me? (*Without a word* SHE *goes back to stage right.*) Wait! (SHE *stops.*) Why must I get down on my knees?

SHE: Because I did before.

DADDY: Me? In front of you?

SHE: No. Me in front of you.

DADDY: It wouldn't look right.

SHE: Now it's your turn.

DADDY: I warn you. There are limits. . . .

SHE (*approaches* DADDY *and puts down her carry-all*): Don't be afraid. Down on your knees.

DADDY: Because if I do . . .

SHE: Nothing will happen to you. I know what I'm doing. Trust me.

DADDY: This is going to end badly. (*Sinks down on his knees. Pause.*) Now what?

SHE: Nothing.

DADDY: But what comes next?

SHE: Do you realize that you look stupid?

DADDY: Didn't I tell you?

SHE: Absolutely ridiculous.

DADDY: In that case I'll get up.

SHE: In that case I'm leaving.

DADDY: Then what have I got to do?

SHE: There's only one way out.

DADDY (*hopefully*): What?

SHE: Only one word can save your honor. There's only one word you can say when you're on your knees to me. Only one word that you *must* say if you don't want to look stupid in this situation.

DADDY (*with suspicion*): What are you driving at?

SHE: Don't be so innocent.

DADDY: This is a trap.

SHE: Until you've said it, you'll continue to look *very* stupid. (*Pause.*) Well? (*Pause.*) What? You can't? I'll help you. (SHE *starts to laugh.*)

DADDY: Stop that!

SHE: I can't. It's too funny. . . . Zeus on his knees, Kilimanjaro . . . Daddy . . . (SHE *laughs.*)

DADDY: Stop. I . . . I'll say it.

SHE: Well, what are you waiting for? (*Pause.* DADDY *mumbles something unintelligible.*) Louder! (DADDY *mumbles again.*) I don't hear a thing!

DADDY (*bellows*): I'm in love!

SHE: With whom?

DADDY (*bellows*): With you!

SHE (*affecting surprise*): With me?

DADDY (*bellowing*): With you, with you, with you! Are you satisfied?

SHE (*unbending*): You mean you love me?

DADDY (*resigned, feebly*): I love . . .

SHE: See?

DADDY: I'm not ridiculous anymore?

SHE: Just a minute! Swear it!

DADDY: Swear what?

SHE: That you love only me!

DADDY: Yes. Only you . . .

SHE: . . . that you've never loved anyone as much as me.

DADDY: Do I have to?

SHE: Oh, so you're not sure?

DADDY: No, no, I'm sure.

SHE: Then why the hesitation? (*Pause.*) I'm waiting.

Pause.

DADDY: All right. I swear.

Three cuckoo calls are heard outside.

SHE: What's that?

DADDY (*stands up and dusts his knees with his sleeve*): A cuckoo.

SHE: How do you know?

DADDY: Because I heard it.

SHE: But why does it go cuckoo?

DADDY: Because it's a cuckoo.

SHE: Maybe it's warning us. (DADDY *carries her carry-all back into the corner, stage right rear.*) I'm afraid. I feel funny. (SHE *stands on one foot, holding her other ankle in both hands.*)

DADDY: What are you doing?

SHE: Feeling my pulse.

DADDY: That's not the place. Give me your hand.

SHE: I'm sure I have a fever.

DADDY (*taking her wrist; pause*): Perfectly normal.

SHE: It's my nerves. I'm on edge.

DADDY: What's wrong with you exactly?

SHE (*leaning against him*): I feel so weak. . . .

DADDY (*supporting her, worried*): It will pass.

SHE: You're so experienced.

DADDY: A common headache.

SHE: So wise . . .

DADDY: Come. You'd better lie down.

He tries to lead her to the sofa, but SHE *almost falls, whereupon* DADDY *picks her up in his arms. He is visibly worried.*

SHE: . . . and so strong . . .

DADDY *settles her on the sofa.*

DADDY: Drink something. It will do you good.

He takes the bottle and a glass from the table.

SHE: But only a drop.

DADDY *hands her the glass.* SHE *empties it at one gulp.*

DADDY: And now close your eyes. Relax. That's it. (*He stretches out her legs on the couch and sits down be-*

*side her with the bottle in his hand. For a moment the
light has been dimming almost imperceptibly. The
blue of the sky grows darker.)* Listen to the silence.
The sun is setting, the cuckoos are going to bed, they
won't frighten my baby anymore. Everywhere silence,
peace . . .

*In the distance, a shot is heard, followed by a long
drawn-out echo.*

SHE (*with a start*): What's that?
DADDY: A hunter.
SHE: My heart's going pit-a-pat.
DADDY: There's nothing to worry about.
SHE: But why is he shooting?
DADDY: Don't think about it.
SHE (*lying down again*): Then tell me a story.
DADDY: About what?
SHE: Tell me about *you.*

Pause.

DADDY: I don't know where to begin. . . .
SHE: Oh, just in general. That's the easiest way.
DADDY (*begins in a solemn tone*): In the present era . . .
SHE: Did you have a bear?
DADDY: A bear?
SHE: A teddy bear. (SHE *pulls his ear, squealing with affec-
tion.*) My little teddy bear!
DADDY: Ouch, you're hurting me!
SHE: You have no imagination. Are you capable of dream-
ing?

DADDY: It's been so many years.

SHE: Does it pass with age?

DADDY (*offended*): Not with age. With time.

SHE: Same difference.

DADDY: Not at all. There was a time when people dreamed even with their eyes open.

SHE: Of what?

DADDY: Of great things.

SHE (*pulls him by the sleeve and hands him her empty glass*): Just a tiny bit more.

DADDY (*pouring*): The world was different then. More romantic. More spiritual. We dreamed of glorious deeds.

SHE: What kind of deeds?

DADDY: Historical.

SHE: How deliciously exciting! (SHE *drains her glass at one gulp and sets it down on the floor.*)

DADDY: . . . of distant goals, great transformations . . .

SHE: Go on! Go on! (SHE *takes the bottle from him and puts it to her lips.* SHE *notices that* DADDY *has fallen silent.*) Why did you stop?

DADDY: There's nothing more to say.

SHE: That's not true. (SHE *drinks again.*)

DADDY: No, really. It's all dead. I don't even know whether it's good or bad. . . . (*He claps his hand to his mouth pretending to be horrified at what he has said.*) What am I saying! Of course it's good!

SHE (*setting the bottle on the floor*): What?

DADDY: That it's gone.

SHE: That what's gone?

DADDY: I've just been telling you. Are you listening?

SHE (*slightly tipsy*): My poor darling. Did you love her very much?

DADDY: Who?

SHE: That woman?

DADDY: What woman?

SHE: You loved her, didn't you?

DADDY: Her?

SHE: You can tell me about it. I understand.

DADDY: Her?

SHE: I see it all clearly. What became of her?

DADDY: She . . . all right. (*He laughs.*) She died.

SHE: Stop that!

DADDY: All right. All right. I've stopped. I'm serious. (HE *chokes with laughter.*)

SHE: I understand. You laugh because you're suffering.

DADDY (*gaily*): Exactly . . .

SHE: When . . . was it?

DADDY: Oh, quite a while ago. You were still a child.

SHE: I understand and I forgive you. (*Seriously and with emotion.*) There are experiences we can only bear to remember if we keep our distance from them. And the best way to do that is with irony and laughter, but it's a laughter that verges on tears. You must have been very unhappy.

DADDY: Yes. That is . . .

SHE: Desperate . . .

DADDY: Well . . .

SHE: Lost.

DADDY: Yes, in a way.

SHE (*cries out impatiently*): Were you unhappy or weren't you?

DADDY (*eagerly*): Yes, yes, of course. You're perfectly right.

SHE (*softening*): Come here to me. (*Puts her arm around him.*) My poor, poor boy!

DADDY (*with enthusiasm*): Yes, yes, I am a poor boy.

SHE: Poor, tired, dear heart . . . Come here and rest.

> SHE *draws him to her and together they roll on the floor. They speak the following speeches rolling on the floor in an embrace.*

DADDY (*rolling*): That's it, dear little heart!

SHE: Lost, sad . . .

DADDY (*happier and happier*): Sad? Oh yes, very sad!

SHE: I'll console you for all your suffering. . . . (*A cuckoo call is heard behind the window.* SHE *jumps to her feet.*) Again!

DADDY (*sits up, rather dazed*): What is it?

> *Another cuckoo call.*

SHE: Do you hear?

DADDY: Oh yes, the cuckoo.

> *He stands up and tries to take her in his arms. A third cuckoo call.*

SHE (*repulsing him*): No, no, I can't. That bird bothers me.

DADDY (*furious*): That's no bird. That's a pest.

> *He runs to the window and closes it with a crash, and also closes the shutters of both windows. The room is in total darkness.*

SHE: Where are you?

DADDY: Here.

SHE: I can't see a thing.

DADDY: Wait, I'm coming.

SHE: Light the lamp.

DADDY: No, we don't need the lamp.

The sound of an overturned chair and a muffled curse.

SHE: What's that?

DADDY: I'm sorry. It really is dark.

> DADDY *strikes a match. He limps over to the lamp and lights it. There is a third person in the room—*THE GHOST*—who is standing beside the door, stage right. The face, including the eyebrows, is white. Thick black circles are painted around the eyes. Abundant flaming red hair in a provocative, pretentious hair-do. It covers the forehead and descends in curls over the shoulders. The rest of* THE GHOST *is hidden by a long, wide, black cape that reaches to the ground.*

THE GHOST (*in a deep voice*): Good evening.

DADDY: Who are you?

THE GHOST: I'm not intruding?

DADDY: How did you get here?

THE GHOST: The door was open.

DADDY: That's no reason for coming in.

THE GHOST: I wished to speak to you.

DADDY (*to* SHE): Do you know her?

SHE: Do you?

> *Pause.*

DADDY: Please leave. (THE GHOST *does not react.* DADDY *puts on his bowler—which had fallen off while he was roll-*

ing on the floor—pulls it down over his forehead, and straightens his jacket.) Please leave! (THE GHOST *does not react.*) Kindly leave this house at once! (THE GHOST *does not react.*) Get out! (*Slowly* THE GHOST *goes to the couch and sits down.* DADDY *to* SHE.) What should I do?

SHE: I think I'll be going. (SHE *starts stage left.*)

THE GHOST: Don't go. I should like a word with you, too. (SHE *stops.*)

DADDY: Then I'll go. (*He starts stage right.*)

THE GHOST: As you wish, sweetheart.

DADDY (*stops*): Are you addressing me?

THE GHOST: Don't you recognize me?

SHE: What—you know him, Madam?

THE GHOST (*to* SHE): And you, Miss, don't you know me?

DADDY (*to* THE GHOST): We don't know each other.

THE GHOST (*to* SHE): Then let's get acquainted.

SHE: What for?

THE GHOST: When I tell you how I met him——

SHE (*to* DADDY): You never told——

THE GHOST: No, he never will.

DADDY (*to* THE GHOST): See here——

SHE: A pretty kettle of fish!

DADDY: What's that?

SHE: Is this any way to treat me?

THE GHOST (*to* DADDY): Tell the young lady——

DADDY: There's nothing to be told.

THE GHOST: You don't say!

SHE: Will someone kindly tell me——

DADDY (*to* SHE): What do you think I've been doing?

SHE: Don't take that tone with me.

THE GHOST: Young lady, I will speak. . . .

DADDY (*contemptuously*): I can imagine what she's going to say!

SHE: Will somebody finally say something?

DADDY: Idiot!

THE GHOST: You think I won't speak? You'll see!

SHE: What did you say!

DADDY: I wasn't referring to you.

THE GHOST: I will speak. . . .

DADDY: High time!

SHE: I've had enough!

> SHE *runs out, stage left, slamming the door. Pause.* DADDY, *bewildered, goes stage left, hesitantly presses the door handle, but the door is already locked. He knocks.*

DADDY: It's me. (*Pause.*) Open up. (*No answer.*) It's all a misunderstanding. I'll explain. (*Pause.*) Let me in! (*Pause. He knocks again.*) Only half a second... (*Pause.* DADDY *to himself.*) She's angry. (*He comes back from the door.*) It's all your fault. (*Violently.*) Couldn't you have come at some other time? (THE GHOST *doesn't answer. Furious,* DADDY *approaches.*) Who are you anyway?

> THE GHOST *stands up and takes off his wig, drops his cape, and tosses them both on the sofa. His whole head is smooth and white like his face. He is wearing an olive-drab uniform, without belt, epaulettes, or pockets. His jacket has a high stiff collar that squeezes his neck. Glistening black boots. White gloves.*

THE GHOST: Do you know me now?

DADDY (*retreating*): No, sir.... (THE GHOST *turns around and takes the frame from the wall. He puts the empty frame over his face as though showing a portrait.*)

THE GHOST: It is I!

DADDY: Sun of the fatherland!

THE GHOST (*prompting him*): Hurricane of glory!

DADDY: Father of victory! Savior! Man of providence, inspired thinker, glorious teacher, eagle of history... (DADDY *comes to attention.*) Beloved Leader!

THE GHOST: At last you recognize me.

> *He hangs the frame on the wall. Pause. They face each other motionless,* DADDY *at attention, chest thrust out, his thumbs to his trouser seams. After a moment* DADDY *slowly recoils.*

DADDY: You're nothing but a ghost.

THE GHOST: That's a lie.

DADDY: A shadow.

THE GHOST: Lies!

DADDY (*raising his voice*): A phantom, an apparition. Nothing more!

THE GHOST (*apoplectic with rage*): Lies, lies! How dare you ... you miserable idiot, you insignificant grain of dust ... I'll ... men like you ... I've sent millions of them to ... (*He raises both hands to his face.*) You're right. I'm only a ghost. (*He lets his hands drop and sits down in a chair.*)

DADDY: You see? (*Pause.*) You've sure changed, Chief.

THE GHOST: What do you expect? I'm dead.

DADDY: Then what have you come here for?

THE GHOST: You don't seem pleased. . . .

DADDY: Don't get me wrong, Chief. I'm delighted to see you. But, no offence, is there any point in our meeting? Each man to his business. One's dead, the other's alive. I'm not one to interfere with anybody's eternal rest. Live and let die. That's my motto.

THE GHOST: You people have short memories.

DADDY: Don't make trouble for me, Chief. Things change. I move with the spirit of the times, and the spirit of our times isn't your spirit, Chief.

THE GHOST: Spirit of the times! Times without spirit, you mean.

DADDY: Possibly. In any case you haven't survived yourself.

THE GHOST: Because you, the living, didn't want me to.

DADDY: But why do you come around haunting people, meddling in their affairs?

THE GHOST: You don't want to remember.

DADDY: There you go again.

THE GHOST: You've begun to forget.

DADDY: Wouldn't it be better to rest in peace when you have the chance?

THE GHOST: Try it yourself. You'll see.

DADDY: I'm not in the mood.

THE GHOST: I was too great for you.

DADDY: But you've shrunk. Forget it. We parted without regrets and now it's time for each of us to go—or lie—his own way. Why stir up ancient history?

THE GHOST: Come closer. (*Reluctantly* DADDY *comes closer.*) Closer! . . . Take off your hat. (*Slowly* DADDY *takes off his hat.*) Hm. Bald.

DADDY: Only superficially.

THE GHOST: Double chin, paunch, eyes without luster. You're not what you used to be.

DADDY: I'm not complaining.

THE GHOST: You used to be different: Red cheeks, elastic step, fire in your eyes . . .

DADDY: What can we do? Youth . . .

THE GHOST: It wasn't just that. Love . . .

DADDY: No, no!

THE GHOST: You loved me.

DADDY (*violently*): Let's not be sentimental.

THE GHOST: Ah, that got under your skin!

DADDY: I forbid you!

THE GHOST: Oh yes, my friend. It was love. You can't change that. You loved me.

DADDY (*with reticence*): Let's say I had a liking for you.

THE GHOST: What, you've forgotten your passion?

DADDY: Well, maybe there was something.

THE GHOST: Not "something"! Passion!

DADDY: Let's not exaggerate.

THE GHOST: I have proof.

DADDY: For instance?

THE GHOST: For instance, a certain moment: I'm standing on the balcony and you down below, looking up at me. Just a little sign from me was enough to make you shout with joy. You were ready to die for a sign from me.

DADDY: You really believe that?

THE GHOST: You shouted, didn't you?

DADDY: It was an order.

THE GHOST: And when you took the oath?

DADDY: When?

THE GHOST: That same day. On the square.

DADDY: Everybody took the oath.

THE GHOST: But you spoke the words.

DADDY: In unison.

THE GHOST: Unless I'm very much mistaken it was your own lips that spoke. Your burning lips that murmured the oath.

DADDY: A lot of other people were murmuring.

THE GHOST: Not all the same thing. Your father, for instance.

DADDY (*violently, pulling his hat down over his head*): Leave me alone!

THE GHOST: Do you remember your father?

DADDY: An elderly man? Tall and well built?

THE GHOST: That's it. You must have known him.

DADDY: I remember him vaguely.

THE GHOST: He didn't like me.

DADDY: Really? It's possible.

THE GHOST: What became of him?

DADDY: He must be dead.

THE GHOST (*with a sigh*): Ah, just as I thought. Poor man, he wasn't strong. He didn't care for darkness. I'm sure he preferred open spaces, sunny vistas. . . . But I'm not telling you anything new. You must know. You knew him better than I did.

DADDY: No, no. Why? He liked the darkness. . . .

THE GHOST: I think you're mistaken. He disliked me, but he disliked the darkness even more. You knew that, didn't you?

DADDY: I believe he hated you most.

THE GHOST: You may be right. If he had hated the darkness more, he wouldn't have said he hated me. But since he liked the cold and the darkness better than me, he didn't hide his dislike for me. And when his words came to your ears, you obliged him by helping him to move into the darkness. Is that it?

DADDY: M-more—or less—

THE GHOST: I can only compliment you on your filial solicitude. But then the darkness must have incommoded him, because he died. Consequently there's still another possibility.

DADDY: Drop it, Chief. It's too complicated.

THE GHOST: On the contrary. It's very simple. Your father didn't like me and you didn't like your father. Why? It's obvious: because he didn't like me. It follows that you loved me.

DADDY: No!

THE GHOST: It's also possible that you loved me because your father hated me and you hated your father. But that amounts to the same thing. In any case, you loved me . . .

DADDY: Stop it, Chief, stop it.

THE GHOST: . . . because if you hadn't loved me, you wouldn't have put your own father in prison for disliking me. No, my good friend, such things are done only for love.

Pause.

DADDY: What do you want of me?

THE GHOST: A mere trifle.

DADDY: Make it quick. I've had enough.

THE GHOST: Love me again.

Pause.

DADDY: Impossible.

THE GHOST: Why?

DADDY: Because . . . because you're dead.

THE GHOST: What difference does that make? I admit I
haven't been in the best of form recently, but love
doesn't worry about beauty. That's why I turn to you.
Just love me; you'll see that the rest will take care of
itself. That's all I'm asking of you.

DADDY: Is it necessary to you?

THE GHOST: Don't you understand the situation I'm in? Being dead is nothing. There are worse things . . . little
by little I'm being forgotten. They've even thrown my
portrait on the junkpile. Some memory of me lingers
here and there, but it's growing dimmer and dimmer.
It barely enables me to rise from my grave and take a
few steps . . . And look at the state I'm in . . . a ghost,
a phantom . . . transparent as a memory that's fading,
growing paler and paler. And every night I feel more
feeble. One of these midnights I won't be able to rise
from the grave, I won't have the strength. I'll lie inert,
just listening, and if I cry out, no one will hear me.
And then that, too, will end. There won't be anything
left. I'll turn to nothingness.

DADDY: What can be done?

THE GHOST: Love does wonders. If a faded memory has suf-
ficed to make me stand here before you, what won't

love do? It will bring me back to life. Give me your
love and I'll rise from the dead. Just give me your love.

DADDY: But I can't.

THE GHOST: You shouted: "Long live!" Prove to me now
that you were sincere. This is your chance.

DADDY: Believe me, Chief——

THE GHOST: I believed you then. Remember your oath.

DADDY: That was a long time ago.

THE GHOST: Can it be that you're unfaithful?

Pause.

DADDY: No. How could you——

THE GHOST: Can you have deceived me?

DADDY: Me? Deceive you? Never!

THE GHOST (*stands up, indicates the door on the left*): And
that woman?

Pause.

DADDY: She . . . she's my daughter-in-law.

THE GHOST (*shouts*): Don't lie! I know everything.

DADDY: You were watching us?

THE GHOST: I saw a thing or two.

DADDY: Appearances can be deceptive. . . .

THE GHOST: So that's your spirit of the times, you old rake.
You're old enough to be her grandfather.

DADDY: A moment of weakness . . .

THE GHOST: Cheat!

DADDY: A passing fancy . . .

THE GHOST: Liar!

DADDY: I forgot myself!

THE GHOST: I saw you on your knees to her.

DADDY: A chain of circumstances . . .

THE GHOST: I heard you swear . . .

DADDY: She demanded it. . . .

THE GHOST: That's no excuse. Who was it who assured me, who gave me his promises, his solemn word of honor, that he would be faithful to me for all time? Who swore an oath to me?

DADDY: Pipe down, for God's sake. She's listening . . .

THE GHOST: Splendid! Let her hear! Let her know what there was between us! I have nothing to hide from her!

DADDY: It will make her unhappy . . .

THE GHOST: Do you think I don't suffer when you're with another?

DADDY: You a sweetheart, Chief?

THE GHOST: A bride!

DADDY: A slightly faded one.

THE GHOST: That's beside the point. I claim my right. I will not permit you to be unfaithful to me with any spirit of the times, I——

DADDY: Very well . . . in that case . . . it's all over between us.

Pause.

THE GHOST (*taken aback*): What did you say?

DADDY: I don't want to see you anymore!

THE GHOST: Are you serious?

DADDY: Never again. It's time to part. Forever.

THE GHOST: You'd better think it over.

DADDY: I've thought it over.

THE GHOST: It's irrevocable?

DADDY: Why beat about the bush? There's someone in my life. Look somewhere else for love. I take back my promise.

THE GHOST: You're going to forsake me?

DADDY: Goodbye forever.

THE GHOST: You may be sorry . . .

DADDY: No, I have no regrets.

THE GHOST: Lover, come back to me.

DADDY: Our love was never meant to be . . .

THE GHOST: Baby, please don't leave me.

DADDY: I have nothing more to say to you.

THE GHOST: Do you remember the day our love was born . . . ?

DADDY: Remember that the best of friends must part. (THE GHOST *falls on his knees.* DADDY *in confusion.*) Don't, Chief . . . it doesn't look right, you, in front of me. . . .

THE GHOST: Give me back your heart.

DADDY: Stand up, Chief.

THE GHOST: Look! Here I am on my knees . . . I, whom you groveled to.

DADDY: Don't . . . don't . . .

THE GHOST: By the memory of your father, I implore you: love me again.

DADDY: Stop it! I can't!

THE GHOST: Oh yes, you can. I know your heart still beats for me. If only you wanted, we'd be together again.

DADDY: No, it's finished.

THE GHOST: All is not lost. All you need is the courage to be true to your heart.

DADDY: Tempter!

THE GHOST: You and I together, like in the old days . . .

DADDY: Oh God, the torment!

THE GHOST: Like in the old days. Remember?

DADDY: No.

THE GHOST: Your leader implores you!

DADDY: Onward to victory together!

THE GHOST: At last I recognize you, my falcon!

DADDY: Raise high the banner!

THE GHOST: You still love me!

SHE (*entering, left*): Would you kindly introduce me to the gentleman?

ACT II

The same scene. THE GHOST *has stood up.*

SHE (*in a drawing-room tone*): Would you kindly introduce me to the gentleman?

DADDY: My daughter-in-law ... my ... an old friend.

SHE (*holding out her hand to* THE GHOST): Pleased to meet you.

DADDY (*suspiciously*): Perhaps you've heard of him?

THE GHOST: You weren't born yet, my dear, when your father-in-law and I ...

SHE: I'm delighted to make your acquaintance. So you've dropped in. ...

DADDY: You must have heard.

SHE: Daddy, don't interrupt. The gentleman and I are conversing.

THE GHOST: To renew an old friendship.

SHE: How sweet of you!

DADDY: I didn't invite him.

SHE: Don't be rude, Daddy. (*To* THE GHOST.) I'm really glad to see you.

THE GHOST: Do you mean that?

SHE: Does it surprise you?

THE GHOST (*looking at* DADDY): Some people have it in for me.

DADDY: Perhaps.

SHE: Who would have it in for anyone so charming?

THE GHOST: Charming?

SHE: You've got something.

DADDY: But . . . but he's a vampire!

SHE: Daddy's always like that. Don't mind him. His manners are rather crude.

DADDY: You talk too much.

SHE: Daddy, we have a guest. . . .

DADDY: I forbid you to speak to strangers!

SHE: The gentleman isn't a stranger. You told me yourself you were old friends.

DADDY: But you don't know him!

SHE: I trust your friends.

DADDY: I don't.

SHE (*to* THE GHOST): Would you care for a cup of tea?

THE GHOST: To tell you the truth, I've come for other reasons.

SHE: Something urgent?

THE GHOST: I wished to talk——

SHE: We'll talk over a cup of tea. Isn't that simpler?

THE GHOST: But . . . you see, I don't drink. For reasons of . . . lifelessness.

SHE: Oh yes, I forgot. Then we'll pretend it's not tea. I won't drink any either.

THE GHOST: If you insist . . . I mean, if it's not too much trouble . . .

SHE: Daddy, be sweet. Go make the tea.

DADDY: Why me?

SHE: Because I'm entertaining our guest. You've done enough talking.

DADDY: But maybe he doesn't want you to entertain him.

SHE: Of course he does. Don't you?

THE GHOST: To be perfectly frank——

SHE: You see, he adores it.

DADDY: I'll ask him.

SHE: Maybe you'd like me to tell you something first?

DADDY (*without assurance*): Uh . . . no, why?

SHE: I thought you wanted to talk to me?

DADDY (*in a panic*): No, no. I'm going.

He goes out, left.

SHE: Won't you be seated? (*They sit down. Pause.*)

THE GHOST (*after clearing his throat*): I am obliged to bring up a painful subject.

SHE (*interrupting*): So you're a ghost?

THE GHOST: The fact is that lately——

SHE: A phantom?

THE GHOST: Unfortunately.

SHE: Why "unfortunately"? What's wrong with it?

THE GHOST: It hampers me. But that's not what——

SHE (*interrupting*): It must be an extraordinary feeling.

THE GHOST: It's quite usual in the afterlife. But getting back to our subject. There's a certain circumstance which——

SHE (*interrupting*): Is it painful?

THE GHOST: What? The circumstance?

SHE: No. Being a ghost.

THE GHOST: No, it's not painful. It's more that something's missing.

SHE: What?

THE GHOST: Something. There's always something missing.

Myself, perhaps. Here, inside. Do you understand? But getting back to our subject——

SHE (*interrupting*): Then you are in pain?

THE GHOST: Yes, in a way. There's a feeling of suction.

SHE: Do tell me about it.

THE GHOST: How can I explain . . . ? I always feel as if something were sucking me in. Eternity, no doubt. And the worst of it is that it's inside me. If it were outside, I could handle it.

SHE: Really? It's inside you and it sucks you in?

THE GHOST: Something like that.

SHE: Fascinating!

THE GHOST: It's only the truth. But that's not what I wanted to——

SHE (*interrupting*): But haven't you ever tried to get even?

THE GHOST: With eternity?

SHE: Yes. To suck it in instead of letting it——

THE GHOST: But I've just told you it's inside me. I can't suck myself in.

SHE: That does make things difficult.

THE GHOST: If you don't mind, I wished to speak with you about something else. About your father-in-law.

SHE: You're wonderful.

THE GHOST: Me?

SHE: Marvelous!

THE GHOST: What makes you think so?

SHE: Because you're so different.

THE GHOST: Yes, that's a fact.

SHE: So spiritual . . .

THE GHOST: That's undeniable.

SHE: So . . . astral . . .

THE GHOST: A little too much so.

SHE: That's just what's so wonderful.

THE GHOST: Are you joking?

SHE: I love it. I've always dreamed of meeting a ghost. Do you know, sometimes I've dreamed of meeting somebody just like you. All men are the same nowadays: normal, human, and so . . . tactile. All alike. It's so monotonous. Nothing happens. They're such bores. You may not believe me, but even Daddy has been a disappointment to me.

THE GHOST: That doesn't seem possible.

SHE: Oh yes. Daddy is Daddy and nothing else. I expected to have an unusual experience with him. Just because he's a daddy. I thought something would happen. That he'd go mad. Or kill himself, or something . . . anyway, something really wild. Something great, something magnificent! Do you understand me?

THE GHOST: Yes, yes!

SHE: But the whole thing is a flop. He'll swallow anything. And to make matters worse he tells me not to be shocked, that everything's normal. He makes everything so commonplace. No, with Daddy it's hopeless.

THE GHOST: I agree. He's always been a groundling. I did all I could to raise him up to my stature. I didn't succeed. He was small and he still is.

SHE: Oh, I'm so glad you understand.

THE GHOST: I understand better than you think. We both tried to do the same thing. We both tried to make something great out of Daddy, to raise him above his daddyness, his mediocre virtue. I almost succeeded.

SHE: How did you go about it?

THE GHOST: I used strong medicine. But he dilutes everything with his daddyism. Even a great crime. Once he did something pretty bad. He did it for me! But it wasn't any use because he forgot it right away. He just pretended nothing had happened. Our virtuous Daddy turns his back on his own crimes.

SHE: Was Daddy a criminal?

THE GHOST: No, because he denied it. He missed his chance.

SHE: Exactly. That's him all over.

THE GHOST: We have our troubles with him.

Pause.

SHE: There's something I want to ask you. But you must tell me the truth.

THE GHOST: I'll do my best.

SHE: The whole truth. Do you promise?

THE GHOST: I'll try.

SHE: Trying won't do. I've got to know definitely.

THE GHOST: All right, I promise.

SHE: Were you a criminal?

Pause.

THE GHOST: Me? That's different.

SHE: What do you yourself think?

THE GHOST: Opinions are divided.

SHE: You promised.

THE GHOST: How shall I put it? I had great plans.

SHE: Were you diabolical?

THE GHOST: Among other things. Above all I had ideas. Magnificent, enormous . . . but the essential is that I was born great. It was my nature.

SHE: You mean that even as a child you——

THE GHOST: No, that's not what I meant. Let's put it like this. I had no need of crimes, neither for my greatness nor for my glory. Crimes are for paltry people, for daddies.

SHE: Then in your opinion you weren't a criminal?

THE GHOST: Perhaps incidentally.

SHE: Not on purpose.

THE GHOST: Not really.

SHE: But you were one, weren't you?

THE GHOST: That doesn't matter now.

SHE: Were you or weren't you?

THE GHOST: That's beside the point.

SHE (*rising*): But I want to know!

Pause.

THE GHOST (*rising majestically*): I have been everything! (SHE *closes her eyes and, spellbound, approaches* THE GHOST. THE GHOST, *anxiously.*) What's the matter? (SHE *stands close to him, tilts her head back, and offers him her lips.* THE GHOST *looks around in bewilderment.*) What are you doing . . . ? (SHE *throws her arms around his neck, trying to force him to kiss her.* THE GHOST *struggles.*) Let me go. It's not my . . . dimension.

SHE *finally succeeds in more or less pressing herself against* THE GHOST, *who has stopped resisting.* DADDY *enters, stage left, carrying three cups and saucers and a sugar bowl on a tray. He stops for a moment and observes the scene.*

DADDY (*icily*): The tea is ready.

> SHE *and* THE GHOST *separate in embarrassment.* SHE *goes upstage, takes out a mirror and arranges her hair.* THE GHOST *stands motionless, at a loss.* DADDY *sets the tray down on the table.*

THE GHOST (*with affected gaiety, rubbing his hands*): Ah, the tea. (*All are silent.*) Well, let's sit down. (SHE *takes out a comb and fixes her hair, turning her back on the others.* DADDY *stands motionless, resting both hands on the table edge.* THE GHOST *approaches the table, sits down opposite him, picks up a cup, takes sugar, stirs his tea a little too energetically, producing a tinkling sound. His eyes meet* DADDY's *stare. The tinkling of his teaspoon gradually dies down and stops. A moment's silence.*) Why doesn't somebody say something? (DADDY, *still leaning on the table edge, stares at him fixedly.*) You won't believe me ... (DADDY *leans slightly toward* THE GHOST, *looking daggers at him.*) It wasn't my fault. ... (DADDY *leans a little further forward.* THE GHOST *hastily.*) A chain of circumstances, a misunderstanding ... (DADDY *leans still further forward.* THE GHOST, *still more precipitatedly.*) A mistake, an accident, a moment of distraction ... (DADDY *is silent, his face almost touching* THE GHOST's.) These things can happen to anybody. ...

DADDY (*forcefully, without raising his voice*): You two-timing corpse.

THE GHOST (*recoiling along with his chair*): I forbid you——

DADDY: You lecherous nightmare—

THE GHOST (*jumping up*): Don't go too far!

DADDY (*straightening up, shouting*): Enough!

THE GHOST: What's got into you?

> *He retreats.* DADDY *takes his umbrella which was hanging on the back of a chair and goes toward him.* SHE *sits down at the table in* THE GHOST's *place and quietly starts drinking his tea.*

DADDY: Now I know what you came for. You thought you could take her away from me with your gravedigger's trick. Oh no, my dear ghost.

THE GHOST: You accuse me unjustly.

DADDY: You graveyard Don Juan!

THE GHOST: Let me explain——

DADDY: You philandering spook!

THE GHOST: Let's not get personal. I refuse to talk in such an atmosphere.

DADDY: You wish I were ten feet under, don't you?

THE GHOST: I only wish you'd take a higher tone. What vulgarity!

DADDY: It bugs you to see me alive.

THE GHOST: It's only a matter of time.

DADDY: But meanwhile I enjoy myself and you're not in on it. Ah, you're drawn to the world, you thought you'd pick a flower from someone else's garden. Is that it, you old dust-biter?

THE GHOST: Slander!

DADDY (*shouting*): Not only old! But dead! Aren't you ashamed of yourself?

THE GHOST (*forced against the wall*): I had my reasons.

DADDY: I'd be glad to hear them—
THE GHOST (*pointing to* SHE): Ask her!

Pause.

DADDY (*turning away from* THE GHOST; *to* SHE): Right. I forgot. There were two of you.
THE GHOST: First hear the truth. Then you can accuse me.
DADDY: What do you mean?
THE GHOST: Between gentlemen: nothing.
DADDY: Very well. I'll ask her.
THE GHOST: Go ahead and ask her. You'll learn some interesting things.
DADDY: About what?
THE GHOST: About yourself. I say no more. She knows best.
DADDY: I'm curious to hear.
THE GHOST: It's high time.
DADDY: But remember. If it turns out——
THE GHOST: I'm not afraid of the truth.
DADDY (*to* SHE): Well, what happened?

Pause.

SHE (*putting down her cup*): He tried to seduce me.
DADDY: Ah-ha!
THE GHOST: What!
DADDY: So that's it.
THE GHOST (*feverishly*): Think, Madam. Remember what you said. Try to remember the course of events. Omit nothing, forget nothing. Recall word for word and sentence for sentence. Have you nothing more to say?
SHE: No.

THE GHOST (*shouting*): Remember!

DADDY (*to* THE GHOST): Isn't that enough for you?

THE GHOST: But what of your dreams, your yearning for a different world, a new spirit, our common endeavors? Is all that nothing?

DADDY (*suspiciously*): What common endeavors?

SHE: I don't know. He's trying to make trouble.

DADDY: First he tries to rape you, then he slanders you!

THE GHOST: Madam, tell the truth!

DADDY (*to* THE GHOST): Look here. Up to now I believed you. I thought you were unhappy, I thought you were sincere when you asked me to come back to you. I was almost ready to fall for it. But now I see what a viper you are. It's all over between us. Don't count on me.

THE GHOST: All is lost!

DADDY (*kisses her hand gallantly*): Thank you!

THE GHOST: What for?

DADDY: For opening my eyes. Now I see it all clearly.

THE GHOST: This is too much!

DADDY: And now we shall abandon you to oblivion. You will slowly disappear. There will be no return. I will give you back to nothingness and go my way.

SHE (*standing up*): Not alone, Daddy. I'll go with you.

DADDY: Naturally.

With his left hand he takes her arm. In his right hand he holds his umbrella. Ostentatiously SHE *leans her head on his shoulder. Slowly they move to stage left.*

THE GHOST: But what about me?

DADDY: You will be privileged to look upon our love.

They go out, stage left. On the way out SHE *waves goodbye to* THE GHOST *with a slight smile.* THE GHOST *looks after them, then makes a gesture of helplessness. He takes his wig and cape under his arm and moves toward the door, stage right. A soft knocking on the right-hand door.* THE GHOST *hurries away from the door, puts on his wig, and wraps himself in the cape. It is important to note that when* THE GHOST *appears in feminine costume the actor playing his part should avoid all gestures or intonations suggesting erotic ambivalence. On the contrary, his voice and movements contrast with his costume by their virility and authority. The knocking is repeated.*

THE GHOST: It's open.

A frail-looking young man enters, or, rather, sticks his head timidly through the aperture: THE LITTLE FELLOW. *Broad, striped tie, navy-blue blazer with silver buttons, tight-fitting beige trousers buttoned below the knees. White stockings and high, black, patent-leather shoes. Long hair. Slung over his shoulder, a shotgun.*

THE LITTLE FELLOW (*timidly*): May I come in?
THE GHOST: It's rather late. But come in.
THE LITTLE FELLOW (*closing the door behind him*): Do you live here, Ma'am?
THE GHOST: I'm visiting. You seem to be a stranger yourself.
THE LITTLE FELLOW: I was lost in the woods. . . .

Pause. THE GHOST *looks him over.*

THE GHOST: Strange. You remind me of someone. (*Making a decision.*) Shall we sit down? (*Shows* THE LITTLE FELLOW *a chair. He himself sits on the other side of the table, showing the audience his right profile.* THE LITTLE FELLOW *takes the proffered chair and sits down at some distance from the table, his right profile turned toward* THE GHOST.) There's still some tea, though it may be a trifle cold. (*He pushes the tray in front of* THE LITTLE FELLOW, *who takes a cup and saucer. Pause.*) So you've been hunting?

THE LITTLE FELLOW: Oh, just a little.

THE GHOST: With what success?

THE LITTLE FELLOW: I . . . none.

THE GHOST: How so?

THE LITTLE FELLOW: I missed.

Pause.

THE GHOST: Are you an experienced hunter?

THE LITTLE FELLOW: I . . . no, this is the first time.

Pause.

THE GHOST: The first time? Then you've done very well. A little more sugar? (*Pause.* THE LITTLE FELLOW *sits straight and stiff.*) Will you permit me a question? Is your father living? (THE LITTLE FELLOW *drops his spoon on the floor. He stands up, puts his cup and saucer down on his chair and gets down on all fours to pick up the spoon. In so doing he bumps into the chair, carefully puts the spoon down on the chair and bends down to pick up the cup. This time he bumps his head against the table. He puts the cup and saucer down on the table and sits down on his spoon. He remains motionless and solemn as before.*) It doesn't matter. There's another. (*He hands another cup and saucer across the table.*) Do forgive me if I seem indiscreet, but isn't it normal to have parents? (THE LITTLE FELLOW *removes the spoon from under his seat, examines it from all sides as if he had never seen it before, and sets it carefully on the floor.*) I asked out of curiosity. You look as if you had parents. (*Pause.*) Well? (THE LITTLE FELLOW *nods.*) Just as I expected. (*Pause.* THE GHOST *examines him attentively.*) I know! Of course! I know whom you remind me of. I'll tell you. Shall I? (THE LITTLE FELLOW *turns with his chair to face* THE GHOST. *His left profile is turned toward the audience.*) Once upon a time I had a friend. Oh, it's true, you don't even know the meaning of "once upon a time." You're too young. (THE LITTLE FELLOW, *still at a certain distance from the table, rises and puts his cup and saucer down on the tray.*) Well, this friend and I spent our best years together. I was very much attached to him. Or rather—he was to me. And I'm sure he was very happy . . . But why am I telling you all this? We don't even know each other. (THE LITTLE FELLOW *unslings his gun and hangs it on the back of his chair.*) Perhaps because of the resemblance . . . but I'm boring you. (THE LITTLE FELLOW *pulls down his jacket and smooths his hair.*) Because you do look like him. You're as much alike as two drops of water. The same eyes, the same features . . . (THE LITTLE FELLOW *buttons his jacket up to his neck, nervously twisting his head.*) The same gestures . . . (THE LITTLE FELLOW *flings himself across the table, trying to throw his arms around* THE GHOST. THE GHOST *dodges his embrace,* THE LITTLE FELLOW *falls on the table, upsetting the cups.* THE GHOST *jumps to his feet.*) What are you doing?

THE LITTLE FELLOW (*feebly*): I . . . adore you . . . Ma'am. (*His head falls and he remains lying on the table with arms outstretched.*)

THE GHOST (*to himself*): This is the pay-off. (*Pause.* THE LITTLE FELLOW *lies motionless.*) Calm yourself, young man. . . . Come, come. Stand up. (*He raises him and leads him to the sofa.* THE LITTLE FELLOW *sits down obediently.* THE GHOST *takes the bottle and glass from the floor, pours cognac, and gives it to* THE LITTLE FELLOW. THE LITTLE FELLOW *drinks and gives back the glass to* THE GHOST *who puts bottle and glass on the table.*) And now I want you to tell me all about it. What brought this on?

THE LITTLE FELLOW: I . . .

From the effects of the alcohol and because he wants to say too much at once, he gags and stammers. THE GHOST *slaps him on the back in a manner that is far from feminine.*

THE GHOST: Take it easy. Plenty of time.

THE LITTLE FELLOW: I saw you this evening. I was in the woods when you appeared. I followed you. . . .

THE GHOST: Was that a nice thing to do?

THE LITTLE FELLOW (*pleading*): Don't be angry, Ma'am. . . .

I saw you enter this house. I didn't dare come in after you. I stayed outside. And now I'm frozen stiff.

THE GHOST: Yes, it's a cool night.

THE LITTLE FELLOW: And then I said to myself that nothing mattered anymore.

THE GHOST: So what do you want of me? A muffler?

THE LITTLE FELLOW (*falls on his knees*): Don't send me away!

THE GHOST: Here's another one down on his knees.

THE LITTLE FELLOW: I've had no peace since the moment I saw you. I've been thinking of you for hours! I can't live without you!

THE GHOST (*to himself*): It runs in the family.

THE LITTLE FELLOW: You're laughing? In that case I'll kill myself. (*He jumps up and runs for his gun.*)

THE GHOST: Forget it, son. You might miss.

THE LITTLE FELLOW (*with dignity*): Then you shoot me!

He hands THE GHOST *the gun.* THE GHOST *takes it, puts it on the table, and begins to pace about the room, deep in thought.* THE LITTLE FELLOW'S *eyes follow his movements.*

THE GHOST: Sit down. (THE LITTLE FELLOW *sits down obediently on a chair.* THE GHOST *continues pacing for a while, then stops.*) My dear boy, I understand that passion makes men blind. But let's be reasonable. In the first place, you don't know women. Putting your whole life in the hands of a woman—it's absurd. It's not worthwhile; what do they amount to? A real man has other aims, spiritual aims. In his eyes love isn't the

profane feeling of one human being for another, of a
man for a woman, or a woman for a man. True love is
the love of an ideal, of some pure thought, some proj-
ect, some abstraction. That is great, pure, spiritual
love. Women? Keep away from them if you want to be
a man.

THE LITTLE FELLOW: You want me to love a spirit?

THE GHOST: Life springs from spirit, never from itself. There
can be no life without spirit, or else you'd have spirit
without life. Never mind, I know what I mean. So I
advise you to find yourself a spirit, not a woman.

THE LITTLE FELLOW: But I don't want to.

THE GHOST: It's for your own good.

THE LITTLE FELLOW: I want to stay with you.

THE GHOST (*impatiently*): And I say: Don't bother me!

THE LITTLE FELLOW: But I don't need a spirit!

THE GHOST: Why not?

THE LITTLE FELLOW: I like you better.

THE GHOST: There you go. You're hopeless. Always the
same old song. Listen to me: I have other reasons for
warning you against women. Women are treacherous.
You can't count on a woman.

THE LITTLE FELLOW: I don't believe it.

THE GHOST: I know from experience.

THE LITTLE FELLOW: You're only saying that to frighten me.

THE GHOST: I have proof.

THE LITTLE FELLOW: That's not possible. You won't betray me.

THE GHOST: I'm not talking about myself.

THE LITTLE FELLOW: Then why say such things?

THE GHOST: As a warning to you. If I were a woman . . .

THE LITTLE FELLOW: Aren't you?

THE GHOST: Superficially. Do you understand?

THE LITTLE FELLOW: No.

THE GHOST: Never mind. I only wanted to make it clear to you how dangerous it is to believe in a woman. Ah, the spirit is something else. The spirit will never betray you. But women? (*He comes closer to* THE LITTLE FELLOW. *In a confidential tone.*) Don't trust them.

THE LITTLE FELLOW (sadly): You don't care for me?

THE GHOST: I like you, and that's why I'm warning you.

THE LITTLE FELLOW (*with enthusiasm*): You will love me!

THE GHOST: I'm trying to tell you there's no point in it.

THE LITTLE FELLOW (*rising*): Let's go then!

THE GHOST: Be still! I do the deciding! (*Pause.*) So you would really follow me?

THE LITTLE FELLOW: To the ends of the earth!

THE GHOST: Right now?

THE LITTLE FELLOW: This minute!

THE GHOST: Good. In that case . . . let's say I agree.

THE LITTLE FELLOW: Oh, thank you, Ma'am.

THE GHOST: Just a minute. But only on condition that you promise me something. I've got to know exactly what I mean to you. I require the certainty that there's no one else in your life, that I am your only passion. Well?

THE LITTLE FELLOW: You don't believe me?

THE GHOST: My dear boy, women just seem to demand such sacrifices. So I advise you to think it over.

THE LITTLE FELLOW: I have thought it over.

THE GHOST: Are you prepared to give up everything?

THE LITTLE FELLOW: To me you are everything.

THE GHOST: And all the others?

THE LITTLE FELLOW: There is no other!

THE GHOST: You've convinced me. Very well. Kindly hand me my things over there in the corner. (*Pointing to the carry-all.*) And let's be going. (THE LITTLE FELLOW *runs eagerly.*) What's the hold-up? (THE LITTLE FELLOW *stands motionless over the carry-all, examining it.*) Are we leaving or aren't we? . . . Did you hear me? . . . What's wrong? (THE LITTLE FELLOW *leans down and rummages feverishly in the carry-all. He takes out a long lace chemise, spreads it out, looks at it, and throws it down.*)

THE LITTLE FELLOW (*turning toward* THE GHOST): Where is she?

THE GHOST: Before I answer your question, I'd like you to confirm my last supposition. Or rather, taking things in their logical order, my first. That suitcase over there. Doesn't it belong to your Daddy? (THE LITTLE FELLOW *turns around, examines the suitcase, and kicks it with all his might.*) Just as I thought.

THE LITTLE FELLOW: Where are they?

THE GHOST: Now I can answer. (*Points to the door on the left.*) There!

THE LITTLE FELLOW *picks up his gun and dashes out, stage left. Pause. In the open doorway, stage left, there appear very slowly: the gun, which* THE LITTLE FELLOW *is hiding behind his back as he slowly retreats, then*

> DADDY, *thrusting out his umbrella and pushing* THE
> LITTLE FELLOW *before him. Looking each other in the
> eye, they enter slowly and rhythmically:* DADDY's *right
> foot, the* LITTLE FELLOW's *right foot, etc.* DADDY, *as
> usual fully dressed, his bowler on his head, makes his
> mustache go up and down. They advance to the cen-
> ter of the stage.*

DADDY (*in a soft voice, but forcefully*): Who gave you permission to take my gun? (*They advance a few steps.*
DADDY, *forcefully, an octave higher, almost chanting.*)
I asked you a question: Who gave you permission to
take my gun?

THE GHOST: I did.

> DADDY *lowers his umbrella and turns toward* THE
> GHOST. *Taking advantage of the diversion,* THE LITTLE
> FELLOW *leans the gun against the nearest chair.*

DADDY: You still here?

THE GHOST: Still? Now I am really here.

DADDY (*to* THE LITTLE FELLOW, *pointing his umbrella at*
THE GHOST): You know him?

THE GHOST: He loves me.

DADDY: What!

THE GHOST: He told me so.

DADDY (*to* THE LITTLE FELLOW): Is that true?

> THE LITTLE FELLOW *nods twice, then shakes his head
> twice, then nods, then shakes his head; in the end he
> wiggles his head as if his collar bothered him.*

DADDY (*to* THE GHOST): Have you been trying to seduce my son?

THE GHOST: If I succeeded with his Daddy . . .

DADDY: Be still. Not in front of the child!

THE GHOST: Why shouldn't he know the history of his family?

DADDY: You can't do this to me.

THE GHOST: To tell you the truth, I like him better.

DADDY (*to* THE LITTLE FELLOW): Don't listen to him! (*He puts his umbrella under his arm and with both hands stops* THE LITTLE FELLOW'*s ears. To* THE GHOST): I forbid you.

THE GHOST: You think you can stop me?

DADDY: I . . . I won't allow it. I'm his father.

THE GHOST: That's good news.

DADDY: I'll speak to him.

THE GHOST: This is something I want to hear.

DADDY (*to* THE LITTLE FELLOW): My unfortunate son, you are falling into evil ways. . . . (*With his forefinger* THE LITTLE FELLOW *gestures toward his ears to indicate that he can't hear.* DADDY *removes his hands and starts in again in a higher pitch.*) My unfortunate son, you are falling into evil ways. How dare you associate with suspicious persons behind my back? What a way to behave! Gadding about at night with God knows who, doing God knows what. Is that a way for a boy of good family to behave? Let me smell your breath? (THE LITTLE FELLOW *complies.*) Exactly. You've been drinking.

THE GHOST: He had a drop with me.

DADDY: You see. Ordinarily I wouldn't mind. The question is: With whom have you been drinking? Innocent child, you don't even know whom you're associating with. In associating with such a person you expose yourself to scandal and you compromise me. This can get 'me into serious trouble. Especially at the present time. Believe me, this fallen ideologism isn't suitable company for you.

THE GHOST: Fallen idol, if you please.

DADDY: It doesn't matter. Fallen in any case. My son, stick to the people who are on top. (*Points to the ceiling.*) That's my advice to you.

THE LITTLE FELLOW: Are you on top, Daddy?

DADDY: I never fall. I know how to regulate my life.

THE LITTLE FELLOW: Then I don't want to be on top.

DADDY: You'd rather be on the bottom?

THE GHOST: I understand him.

DADDY: You prefer the gutter?

THE GHOST (*to* DADDY): He prefers nothing. It's just that he loathes you.

Pause.

DADDY (*offended*): Oh, he loathes me. . . . Isn't that lovely? . . . Me? I suppose I offend his sensibilities. . . . Well, in that case I'll show you what he looks like. (*Points to* THE GHOST.) I know this individual, and now I'm going to show you what's hidden underneath. You thought you'd found a pin-up, didn't you? Well, you're in for a surprise. Watch closely!

He approaches THE GHOST, *puts out his hand to tear off his wig, but before he has time to do so* THE GHOST *does it himself. Pause.*

THE LITTLE FELLOW (*flabbergasted*): Oh, then you're not a lady?

THE GHOST (*throwing off his cape*): I'm not even a gentleman. I am something far more than all women and all men, not to mention children. I am something you've never known because he (*pointing to* DADDY) didn't mention me to you. And do you know why?

DADDY: Because you didn't deserve it, you bungler of history, cursed by all mankind!

THE GHOST: By whom? Did you curse me, when you gave me every assurance of your admiration and loyalty? Or when mingled with a rejoicing crowd you saluted my glory with upraised arm? Or when you paraded, or when you played the informer? Cursed? When? Cursed by you? Don't make me laugh. (*To* THE LITTLE FELLOW.) No, my boy, if he never spoke of me, it's not because he didn't love me. Do you know why it was?

DADDY: Because such things aren't fit for children. Do you expect me to tell him about your crimes? Wouldn't that be nice! My child is innocent. (*He pats* THE LITTLE FELLOW'*s head.*) I refuse to——

THE GHOST: So sensitive!

DADDY: You were a criminal.

THE GHOST: I gave the orders.

DADDY: Some orders!

THE GHOST: And who obeyed them?

DADDY: You had no conscience!

THE GHOST: And who had one but hid it? (*Pause.*) Your conscience comes a little late. It's not exactly an early bird.

DADDY: I did what was ordered.

THE GHOST: And I ordered only what was feasible.

DADDY: Too much!

THE GHOST: That will do. (*Pause. To* THE LITTLE FELLOW.) No, my boy. Your Daddy's trying to wriggle out of it, but in those days the things we did together didn't bother him in the least. He threw himself right into it. It wasn't to spare your innocence that he concealed my existence from you. Do you want to know why it was? Because he's afraid of us. He's worried about his own skin. The old man's afraid because he knows that if we two join forces . . . he'll lose his power .

DADDY: That's a shameless lie!

THE GHOST: Yes, yes. He knows the score. Get him to tell you what we did to his daddy. He was just your age then, and he was on my side. I'm always on the side of the sons. Against the daddies. (*To* DADDY.) Isn't that right, former son of your father?

Pause.

DADDY (*softly but forcefully*): It's *now* that I curse you.

THE GHOST (*to* THE LITTLE FELLOW): Come here, my boy.

THE LITTLE FELLOW *approaches* THE GHOST.

DADDY: Stop.

THE LITTLE FELLOW *stops.*

THE GHOST: I'm going to promise you something.
DADDY: I forbid you!

Pause.

THE GHOST: Perfect. Now I can show you how we handle Daddy and his mania for forbidding. Watch closely, I'll give you a demonstration. (*He steps up to* DADDY, *who is standing stiff and straight with his umbrella at his feet.* THE GHOST *stops in front of him. They are face to face.*) Daddy ... progenitor ... mighty owner of your son. And now ... watch closely! (*With a quick movement he knocks* DADDY'S *bowler down over his eyes.* DADDY *does not react.* THE GHOST *turns to* THE LITTLE FELLOW. *In a boastful tone.*) Well? What do you say? (*Pause.* THE GHOST, *with a quick motion, snatches* DADDY'S *umbrella from his hands and tosses it into a corner. Again he turns to* THE LITTLE FELLOW.) Not bad, eh?

Pause. THE GHOST *gestures to* DADDY *to take off his jacket.* DADDY *slowly complies, with his eyes to the ground. He stands there with bowed head and arms outstretched, holding the jacket by the collar. The bottom of the jacket drags on the floor.* THE GHOST *takes off* DADDY'S *bowler and with a sweeping movement throws it into the corner.* DADDY *does not react.* THE GHOST *grabs him by the vest, shakes him, and gives him to understand that he should also take off his vest.* DADDY *drops his jacket and with both hands un-*

buttons his vest. Before he has finished THE LITTLE
FELLOW *intervenes.*

THE LITTLE FELLOW (*shouting at* THE GHOST): Leave him
alone!

DADDY *stands motionless, his hands on his buttons.*

THE GHOST (*turning to* THE LITTLE FELLOW): What is the
meaning of this?
THE LITTLE FELLOW: Leave him alone!
THE GHOST (*turning back to* DADDY, *ignoring* THE LITTLE
FELLOW): Go on. Step on it.

DADDY *unbuttons and removes his vest. He has on a
white shirt and black trousers too wide at the waist,
held up by suspenders and reaching almost to his
chest. He holds the vest in one hand.*

THE LITTLE FELLOW (*runs over to the gun, picks it up and
aims it at* THE GHOST): Let him go!
THE GHOST: Are you crazy? Can't you see it's your father?
DADDY: Thank you, son. I always knew I could count on
you. (*He puts his vest back on, but does not button it.*)
THE LITTLE FELLOW (*in a fury, pointing the gun at* DADDY):
Shut up, Daddy. (*More softly.*) Don't speak to me.
DADDY: Who do you want me to talk to? (*Indicating* THE
GHOST.) To him?
THE LITTLE FELLOW: Sure, talk to him if you feel like it.
DADDY: I have nothing to say to him.
THE GHOST: My boy, it seems to me ... (THE LITTLE FEL-
LOW *points the gun at him.*) Put that gun down. I'm
losing my patience!

DADDY: Shoot him, my boy! (THE LITTLE FELLOW *points the gun at* DADDY.) All right. I'm not saying a word.

THE GHOST: Fire away. Maybe you'll hit Daddy. You can't hurt me. I'm post-mortal.

DADDY: That's so. You might hurt me. He'd only laugh. You can't kill him.

THE GHOST: I've been through that.

DADDY: Better forget it.

He takes the gun from THE LITTLE FELLOW *and sets it down in the farthermost corner.*

THE GHOST: My boy, I don't understand you. I do what I can to rid you of your father and you defend him. You don't love him, do you?

THE LITTLE FELLOW: I hate him.

DADDY (*raising his arms in a gesture of martyred sanctity*): What do I hear? Is that my reward? Is that a way to talk in the presence of your old father? (*Raising one arm and pointing with his forefinger.*) After all I've done for you . . .

THE GHOST: If you hate him, I'm even more surprised.

Seeing that no one is paying attention to him, DADDY *drops his arm.*

THE LITTLE FELLOW: I hate you, too.

DADDY: Rightly so, my son.

THE GHOST: Me? Why?

THE LITTLE FELLOW: Because.

DADDY: Excellent.

THE GHOST: Don't be childish. Daddy I understand. But me . . . why?

THE LITTLE FELLOW: On account of Daddy.

THE GHOST: Express yourself more clearly.

THE LITTLE FELLOW: You were together.

THE GHOST: Me with him?

THE LITTLE FELLOW: Yes. You with Daddy.

THE GHOST: No. He was with me.

THE LITTLE FELLOW: It's all the same to me.

THE GHOST: I won't argue. But I don't see the connection.

THE LITTLE FELLOW: Because.

THE GHOST: Speak up.

THE LITTLE FELLOW: Daddy loved you.

THE GHOST: And that's enough to make you hate me?

THE LITTLE FELLOW: Yes.

> *Pause.*

THE GHOST: So, if I understand you right, my old friendship with Daddy compromises me in your eyes. Is that right? (THE LITTLE FELLOW *nods his head several times.* THE GHOST *to* DADDY.) Did you hear that? He dislikes me on your account. What do you think of that?

DADDY: He's wrong.

THE GHOST: You mean he ought to like me.

DADDY: No, he's right.

THE GHOST: You mean he's right not to love you?

DADDY: No, not that.

THE GHOST: Make up your mind: Is he right or wrong? Because if he's wrong, it means he ought to love me, and then we'll settle your hash together. But if he's right, it means you're a louse. Take your pick.

Pause.

DADDY: I'm so tired. (*He goes to one side and sits down on a chair.*)

THE GHOST (*to* THE LITTLE FELLOW): Don't be naïve. Daddy doesn't mean any more to me than I do to him.

THE LITTLE FELLOW (*obstinately*): There was something between you.

THE GHOST: Ancient history.

THE LITTLE FELLOW: A love affair?

THE GHOST: A trifle! But now you and I will show the world what it ought to be.

THE LITTLE FELLOW: He worshiped you.

THE GHOST: A passing infatuation. His passion has grown cold.

THE LITTLE FELLOW: But he loved you.

THE GHOST: When you're older, you'll understand how love passes. He stopped loving me, the flame died down. Forget about him. (*To* DADDY.) Isn't it true, old man, that your love has passed? (*Pause.*) You see? He doesn't answer. There's no room left in his heart for love.

DADDY: That's not true.

THE GHOST: You don't say! (*He sits down on a chair.*)

DADDY: Don't believe him, son. It was entirely different. Don't believe him and don't trust him. I'll tell you how it was with us. It's a sad story, but I'll tell it as a lesson to you. I remember . . . he came to see me. I was young then, as fresh as a rose and as innocent. . . . I was impressed by his beauty as you are now. He had

a beautiful moustache and high ideals. He spoke persuasively. He talked eloquently, incomparably. About
his mission, about the destiny of souls, about the radiant future ... (THE GHOST *represses a laugh.*) Well?
Isn't that true?

THE GHOST: Good old Daddy ... go on, keep talking.

DADDY: About the happiness we would share ... he tempted
me, he seduced me. He promised the moon and the
stars. In short, he turned my head.

THE GHOST (*unable to suppress his merriment*): Very good!

DADDY: You mean you didn't take me in?

THE GHOST: Really priceless! ... (*He weeps with laughter
and wipes away the tears.*) Forgive me, my friends, I
can't help it ... what an act!

DADDY: But you admit it's true?

THE GHOST: The diary of a courtesan! Oooh! (*He holds his
sides and doubles up with laughter. But he does not
speak aloud; the sound that issues from him is more
of a squeak.*)

DADDY (*rising suddenly; with pathos*): Yes, I am a courtesan. But who's to blame? Who turned me into a
fallen creature? Who took my virtue and my dignity?
(*Points to* THE GHOST, *who is slapping his thighs,
shaken with irrepressible laughter.*) He! He seduced
me and abandoned me! I couldn't foresee that he'd
abandon me. (*He sits down.*) Let my downfall be a
warning to you, my boy.

THE LITTLE FELLOW: Daddy ... are you crying?

DADDY: I'm crying for you.

THE GHOST (*suddenly breaks off laughing; he rises nimbly;*

he speaks roughly, without a trace of his former gaiety): A moving story. I'll finish it. (*To* THE LITTLE FELLOW.) Do you know why he's crying? Because I didn't pay him enough. First he was all eagerness to give me his virtue, then he saw it didn't pay. The blushing bride expected a higher price. And now she has regrets.

DADDY (*springs up*): No! I did it all for love. You admitted yourself, right here an hour ago, that for you I had even—— (*He interrupts himself and looks in turn at* THE GHOST *and* THE LITTLE FELLOW. *Pause.*) Let's not talk about it. (*He sits down.*)

THE GHOST: Oh no! We've got to talk about it. Now is the time. (*To* THE LITTLE FELLOW.) Enough sentiment. I have a proposition that ought to interest you. Come with me or you will always be your father's slave. He possesses you because he has everything and you have nothing.

DADDY: I gave him life. Isn't that enough?

THE GHOST: What do you call life? (*To* THE LITTLE FELLOW.) Just look at him. So happy to be able to move his belly over the planet. And if he can manage to put it on top of another belly once in a while, his happiness knows no bounds. That's what life means to him: bellihood. And he'd like to fashion you in his image. Do you know why? Because he's only flesh, and as flesh he's stronger than you. If you fight him belly to belly, he'll always win out. That's his strength. He has money and power, law and order, influence and honors. Which help him in turn to other advantages. Am I right, Father-in-law?

DADDY: Demagogue! Provocateur! In the sweat of my brow I——

THE GHOST: He made a law of his way of life, he made a virtue of his age. Just because he's lived a certain number of years, he feels righteous. Legalized and at one with the world, as blissful as a piece of paper after a notary has affixed his stamp: "Certified true copy." Signature, seal, period. And what a distinction not to have been bitten by a microbe in all these years! What shining proof of great wisdom and transcendent virtue! In him, not the microbe.

DADDY: I beg your pardon. I've had the flu.

THE GHOST: How was it?

DADDY: Not bad. I survived.

THE GHOST: But for what did you survive? (*Pause.*) No answer. That's his weak point. That's where we're going to get your Daddy.

DADDY (*alarmed*): Where?

THE GHOST: Against the body I propose the spirit.

DADDY (*relieved*): Oh!

THE GHOST: He doesn't know what he lives for. He's nothing but a body. As a body he'll win, because he's the stronger. But if we attack him in the spirit, we will win. (*To* THE LITTLE FELLOW.) You will, I mean.

THE LITTLE FELLOW: What spirit?

THE GHOST: The spiritual spirit. You need spirit. Only the spirit will break him.

THE LITTLE FELLOW: Who do you mean?

THE GHOST: Me.

DADDY: I was expecting that.

THE GHOST: By yourself you will never be free. You can make faces at him, you can play tricks on him. He'll only laugh. Your rebellion is ridiculous. And that's why I ask you: Will you follow me?

THE LITTLE FELLOW: What have I to gain?

THE GHOST: Let's see: In the first place, certainty. I will give you an answer to all the questions Daddy is unable to answer. In the second place, strength. I will make you a strong man. You will be as hard as a bullet. You will pierce Daddy.

DADDY: Shot with my own son—not bad!

THE GHOST: In the third place, superiority. I will raise you high above Daddy. . . . I will reveal to you Daddy's comings and goings, his sources and motivations. You will look on with indulgence as Daddy bustles about somewhere far below. You will be wiser than he. In the fourth place . . .

SHE (*entering, left*): What are you talking about?

Pause. THE GHOST, DADDY, *and* THE LITTLE FELLOW *turn toward her.* DADDY *stands up and buttons his vest.*

THE GHOST: Ah, our young friend. Greetings! Greetings!

DADDY *moves aside, making himself as inconspicuous as possible.*

SHE (*approaching* THE GHOST *and* THE LITTLE FELLOW): Our little elf! What a pleasant surprise!

THE GHOST: How's the family? All well?

SHE: What's new with you? Still snooping around? (*To* THE LITTLE FELLOW.) I see you know each other. (THE LITTLE FELLOW *says nothing.*) You look a sight!

SHE *straightens his tie and smoothes his hair.*

THE GHOST: He looks dumb.

SHE (*turning to* THE GHOST): What are you doing here exactly?

THE GHOST: Clarifying the situation.

SHE: Did anyone ask you to?

THE GHOST: It's my duty as a friend of the family.

SHE: Aren't you overstaying your welcome?

THE GHOST: We still have things to discuss.

SHE: You and I? I doubt it.

THE GHOST: Not with you. About you.

SHE: I'd like to say something, if you don't mind.

THE GHOST: Go right ahead.

SHE: But not in front of you.

THE GHOST: I won't be offended.

SHE (*to* THE LITTLE FELLOW): Make him go away.

THE GHOST: Tell her to stop shouting.

SHE: Tell him to stop meddling.

THE GHOST: Remember whom you are addressing.

SHE: I can't bear the sight of him.

DADDY: Yes, we'd better go. We'll leave the young people to themselves.

THE GHOST: Be still, Father-in-law. You've said your piece.

THE LITTLE FELLOW (*standing beside* THE GHOST): He will go! (*Pause.*) But with me.

SHE: You're leaving me?

THE LITTLE FELLOW: To Daddy.

THE GHOST: In that case, Madam, you can cheer up. We shall leave. He has understood; there's nothing more to explain.

SHE (*to* DADDY): Daddy, help me.

DADDY: I should prefer not to interfere. . . .

SHE: You're going to let him go with that tramp?

DADDY: I've advised him against it but he won't listen.

SHE: Then forbid him! You're his father!

> SHE *tugs* DADDY *by the sleeve and forces him to face* THE LITTLE FELLOW.

DADDY: For the last time—I'm not speaking for myself but for the family, the basic nucleus of society. So, indirectly, in the name of society, of the common weal . . . Save your family . . . Think of your wife . . . (THE LITTLE FELLOW *takes a step forward.* DADDY *steps back.*) No, better not.

THE GHOST (*putting his hand on* THE LITTLE FELLOW'S *shoulder*): He's thought of everything. (*To* SHE.) You're lucky. Your husband is in good hands. At last your dream will come true. I'll make another man of him. He will be an anti-Daddy. (*To* DADDY.) You can be happy, too. We will fulfill the dream of your youth. Rejoice together! (*To* THE LITTLE FELLOW.) And now follow me!

> *He goes to the right,* THE LITTLE FELLOW *following him.*

DADDY (*to their backs*): Go! Follow him! My order, my hierarchy, my tradition irk you. You hate everything connected with me. Very well! But most of all you hate yourself. Whatever you destroy, you will not escape me, because I created you. Now go! Destroy yourself. Just follow him. He'll show you how it's done.

THE GHOST: We will build our new world without Daddy. (*He opens the door, while* SHE *runs and bars* THE LITTLE FELLOW'S *way.*) We . . . ! (*He breaks off and turns around. He sees that* SHE *is whispering in* THE LITTLE FELLOW'S *ear.* THE LITTLE FELLOW *turns slowly back and sits down in a chair at the center of the stage.*) What did she say?

THE LITTLE FELLOW (*tonelessly*): We're going to have a baby.

Pause.

DADDY (*joyfully*): Maybe a son! (*All approach* THE LITTLE FELLOW. SHE *stops behind him and puts her hands on his shoulders.* DADDY *to stage right of him. On the other side,* THE GHOST, *who has left the door wide open.* DADDY *shakes* THE LITTLE FELLOW'S *limp hand.*) Splendid, my boy. Congratulations! Congratulations!

THE GHOST: Does that mean you're staying?

THE LITTLE FELLOW *makes a gesture of helplessness. Meanwhile* DADDY *kisses* SHE *repeatedly on both cheeks.*

DADDY (*still in his euphoria*): Come to my arms! What a splendid surprise! (THE GHOST *makes a gesture of irritation, moves away, and sits down on the sofa.*) That calls for a drink! We must baptize him! (*Runs to the table, fills two glasses, holds out one to* THE LITTLE

FELLOW, *and raises the other.*) Here's to our children!
(*He sees* THE GHOST *sitting on the sofa.*) What's he
waiting for?

THE GHOST: I'm waiting for him to grow up.

DADDY: If it amuses you. As for me ... (*He empties his
glass, grunts with contentment, and puts it down on
the table.*) I could do with a bite to eat.

SHE: Yes, Daddy. (SHE *leaves* THE LITTLE FELLOW, *puts the
cups on the tray, and goes out, left.* DADDY *takes his
newspaper and his glasses from his suitcase. He sits
down at the table, puts on his glasses, and unfolds the
paper. Seeing that* THE LITTLE FELLOW *is still sitting
motionless, looking blankly around him,* DADDY *goes
up to him and holds out the paper to him.*) It's yes-
terday's ...

THE LITTLE FELLOW *does not react. A cock crow is
heard in the distance.*

THE GHOST (*standing up*): Time for me to go. (*Throws his
cape over his shoulders, hides the wig under his cape.*)
But I'll be back. Tomorrow night. Or the next. I'll
drop in from time to time ... (THE LITTLE FELLOW *sits
motionless;* DADDY *reads his paper.* THE GHOST *stops
behind them and waits. But seeing no reaction, he
moves off to stage right. He stops in the doorway and
says in an explanatory tone.*) Fathers don't like it
when I come.

*He goes out, leaving the door open. In the distance the
second cock crow.* SHE *enters from the left, picks up*

DADDY's *jacket, shakes it, puts it over her arm, and opens the blinds and both windows. A pale cold dawn.* SHE *puts out the lamp and goes out, left.* DADDY *goes on reading the paper.* THE LITTLE FELLOW *continues to stare into space, unaware that he is holding a glass. The third cock crow rings out from directly below the window, very loud.*

Note on the Characters, the Actors, and the Set

All the actors should suit their parts in age and physique. This is especially true of SHE.

THE GHOST is of indeterminate age, but in any case he is no longer young. More important than the actor's age is his "presence." He should have a fine deep voice, but this is not indispensable if his voice is in some other way impressive.

DADDY's costume is inseparable from the character and each part of it has an exact function. Ideally, the actor should be naturally bald or at least have a natural bald spot. If not, it is preferable to avoid the use of a false scalp, unless the artifice can be made imperceptible. A false scalp tends to give an actor a psychopathic look, an effect that is not desired.

The costumes of the young couple include common elements (white stockings, black shoes), suggesting (but not too strongly) a certain uniformity. The author would appreciate attention to this detail. What he absolutely does not wish is that the young couple should represent "the younger generation"; for example, THE LITTLE FELLOW should not appear in blue jeans.

The set should be realistic; for instance, there should be "real" branches behind the windows. No "abbreviations" or "symbols," because there is nothing to abbreviate or symbolize. The scene is neutral and so conventional that there is no need to underline any conventions. All the props should be real objects. The stage should not be cluttered with furniture or props other than those mentioned in the text. Because of the force of expression inherent in every object, any additional element would lend the set meanings that are not in the author's intention.

The walls should be a neutral color like those of exhibition rooms, so as to bring out rather than to blur the outlines and colors of the costumes and props.

THE PROPHETS

Translated by
Ralph Manheim and Teresa Dzieduszycka

Cast of Characters

THE REGENT

THE BAILIFF

FIRST PROPHET

SECOND PROPHET

THREE WISE MEN

    GASPAR

    MELCHIOR

    BALTHAZAR

THE PRIMA DONNA

A monumental hall. Doors to left and right. In the rear, a door opening out on a balcony where THE REGENT *is standing with his back to the audience. He is wearing evening clothes; across his chest a red ribbon with a golden star. His arms are upraised. Backstage are heard the inarticulate cries of a crowd. It is important now and later that these should not be the feeble cries of a few extras, but the sound of thousands of voices, perhaps a recording of an exciting football game.*

THE REGENT (*waving his arms*): Friends and countrymen! (*The cries of the crowd subside gradually.*) Your prayers have been heard! In just a few minutes he will be standing before you. (*Cries of joy, which* THE REGENT *waves down.*) He, the one and only Prophet! He for whom you have been waiting! Even now he is here in the palace. (*Cries of enthusiasm.* THE REGENT *quiets the crowd.*) Braving fatigue and hardship, he has come, just as it was foretold. He has come to you, he has come for you. Prepare to receive him. Open your eyes and ears. Let the blind lend their ears to the deaf and the deaf their eyes to the blind. As for the deaf-blind . . . hmm, never mind. He will appear in person and he himself will proclaim the great news, for he is all-knowing and has fathomed the secret of your future. He will show you the way of salvation. Don't waver in your faith now at the last moment, preserve it as you have preserved it down through the years, as your fathers have done, and your grandfathers. Persevere just a few seconds more, for your cares will soon be ended and your hope will give way to certainty. (*Cries of joy, which* THE REGENT *waves down.*) Now I will step down. I will leave my place in the palace and join you in welcoming him who has come. I lay down the symbols of power that you have entrusted to me for the interim. Let my last proclamation to the people be simply this: The time of your waiting is past!

He takes off his ribbon and throws it down on the square. Cries from the crowd. THE REGENT *turns around, enters the hall, and goes out stage right. The hubbub of the crowd dies down. Pause. The band plays a flourish. From stage right to left enter, at the same time, with a rhythmic, majestic step, two* PROPHETS. *They wear masks which may somewhat resemble the face of Michelangelo's Moses. The masks—beard, high forehead, and the characteristic clump of hair— should be of one piece and appear to be of stone. Purple robes. They hurry to the balcony and collide in the doorway. They look at each other, turn around, and go out from stage left to right faster than they came in.* THE REGENT *comes running and goes out on the balcony.*

THE REGENT: One moment!

He runs out stage right. Pause. Band music. The two PROPHETS *appear to the left and right. They see each*

*other the moment they enter, turn their backs on each
other, and go out again.* THE REGENT *comes running
and goes out on the balcony.*

THE REGENT: Just a second!

*He runs out, mopping his forehead. Pause. At stage
right appears the head of the* FIRST PROPHET. *Having
made sure no one is there, he moves cautiously toward
the balcony. The* SECOND PROPHET *enters from stage
left. On tiptoes he catches up with the* FIRST PROPHET,
*grabs him by the hem of his robe just as he is about to
cross the threshold to the balcony, and, despite his re-
sistance, drags him off-stage. The band strikes up.* THE
REGENT *runs in from stage right.*

THE REGENT (*facing the audience*): Stop that band! (*He
runs out on the balcony.*) Five minutes' intermission.
(*Grumbling of the disappointed crowd.* THE REGENT
returns to the hall.) Hey, Bailiff!

Enter THE BAILIFF, *a sickly-looking, middle-aged man
in a shabby, unbuttoned uniform.*

THE REGENT: What's the meaning of this?
THE BAILIFF: I don't know, Mr. Regent.
THE REGENT: There was only supposed to be one.
THE BAILIFF: It's not my fault. Two of them turned up.
THE REGENT: Which one came first?
THE BAILIFF: Neither, Mr. Regent.
THE REGENT: Express yourself more clearly.
THE BAILIFF: They came together. Only from different di-

rections. Through different doors. I was kind of surprised myself seeing two of them exactly the same, but I said to myself, maybe that's the way it has to be.

THE REGENT: Which of them struck you as ... er, suspicious?

THE BAILIFF: Neither, Mr. Regent. They both look perfectly okay.

THE REGENT: You may leave. (THE BAILIFF *goes toward the door stage left.*) Don't mention this to anyone.

THE BAILIFF: Mum's the word, boss. (*He takes a few steps toward the door.*) Oh, I almost forgot. The Three Wise Men are here.

THE REGENT: Send them in at once! (THE BAILIFF *goes out stage left. In the same doorway appear the* THREE WISE MEN *in traditional but somewhat simplified costume.*)

MELCHIOR: At last!

GASPAR: Congratulations!

BALTHAZAR: We're not too late, I hope.

THE REGENT: I'm afraid I've got bad news for you.

MELCHIOR: He hasn't come?

THE REGENT: On the contrary.

GASPAR: It's all over?

THE REGENT: No, just beginning.

BALTHAZAR: Where is he?

THE REGENT: Where are *they* is the question. Gentlemen, I am grieved to inform you that our expectations have been doubly fulfilled. There are two Prophets.

THE THREE WISE MEN (*in unison*): Impossible!

THE REGENT: It's hard to believe, but facts are facts.

GASPAR: Last time there was only one.

THE REGENT: That proves nothing. This time there are two.

MELCHIOR: It is without parallel in our experience.

THE REGENT: What can I do about it?

BALTHAZAR: There's something definitely wrong. Only one was announced. It's an old tradition. We were called in as experts to welcome——

THE REGENT: You're not telling us anything new, Professor. Obviously there's no sense in having two Prophets. The new truth must be one, or it won't be the truth. The people are expecting only one representative of the truth. Unfortunately . . .

GASPAR: I see no problem. If there are two, one must be false.

THE REGENT: It's not so simple. They're identical.

MELCHIOR: What? Exactly the same?

THE REGENT: Like two peas in a pod.

MELCHIOR: Then both are false, or both are true.

GASPAR: My dear Professor, permit me to point out that you are mistaken. What has no antithesis in truth cannot be false. Moreover, there is no truth without an antithesis in the false. Truth exists only against a background of falsehood. How else could we distinguish it?

BALTHAZAR: Correct.

GASPAR: If the two are the same, it will be difficult to determine which is the right one.

BALTHAZAR: How true!

THE REGENT: So you see what a fix we're in.

MELCHIOR: Let us first inquire whether such a case is possible. Never since the beginning of the world have there been two prophets preaching exactly the same thing.

THE REGENT: That's why I need your advice.

BALTHAZAR: We incline to the view that neither can be true or false, because they are identical. And since there are two of them, neither can be the one and only Prophet.

THE REGENT: Exactly.

MELCHIOR: We shall have to confer.

THE REGENT: But what about the people? They're expecting a Prophet.

MELCHIOR: Find some way of keeping them busy.

THE REGENT: That's not so easy. Quick! This way.

They go out stage right. Enter from stage left THE BAILIFF *and the* FIRST PROPHET.

FIRST PROPHET: Why don't we start?

THE BAILIFF: There's been a delay.

FIRST PROPHET: *I'm* ready.

THE BAILIFF: That's what they all say.

FIRST PROPHET: Tell them if they don't start in five minutes I'm walking out.

THE BAILIFF: *Bon voyage!*

FIRST PROPHET (*stressing each word*): Do you hear me? I am leaving!

THE BAILIFF: Good riddance.

FIRST PROPHET: And I don't want any complaints later.

THE BAILIFF: Never fear.

FIRST PROPHET: I'll wait in the lobby. (*He exits stage left.*)

SECOND PROPHET (*enters from stage left*): Has he gone?

THE BAILIFF: No such luck. (*The* SECOND PROPHET *goes toward the balcony.*) Hey, where do you think you're going?

SECOND PROPHET: I thought I'd take a look at the weather.

THE BAILIFF: The weather's all right. Not raining, not too hot.

SECOND PROPHET: Thank you very much.

THE BAILIFF: Don't mention it.

Pause.

SECOND PROPHET: You're the Bailiff here?

THE BAILIFF: Only recently. I was a carpenter before, I made chairs. But nowadays there's only standing room on earth and all the carpenters have gone broke. That's probably why people are so impatient. Their feet hurt and there's no place to sit down. They're always stepping on one another's toes or trouser cuffs. And every day there are more of us. Did you see the mob on the square?

SECOND PROPHET: Just the right time to appear. I'm ready.

THE BAILIFF: You're not the only one.

THE REGENT *appears on stage right followed by* THE PRIMA DONNA *in a silver-colored, very low-cut dress.*

SECOND PROPHET (*to* THE REGENT): Pleased to meet you. When do we start?

THE REGENT (*evading him*): Excuse me. Later. (*He goes out on the balcony, greeted by cries from the dissatisfied crowd.*) For reasons beyond our control we are obliged to postpone the Prophet's appearance. Meanwhile, we'll have a little entertainment. (*Cries of rage from the square. To* THE PRIMA DONNA.) You're on. (THE PRIMA DONNA *goes out on the balcony and*

launches into a tedious operatic aria. To the SECOND
PROPHET.) And now, what can I do for you?

SECOND PROPHET: I'd like to speak to you alone.

THE REGENT (*to* THE BAILIFF): Leave us. (THE BAILIFF *goes
toward the door stage left.*) Oh yes, while you're about
it, get me my ribbon with the star. I'll be needing it
for a while.

THE BAILIFF: And if they won't give it back?

THE REGENT: Use force.

THE BAILIFF: Easier said than done. (*He exits stage left.*)

SECOND PROPHET: Regent, I wish to protest.

THE REGENT: About what?

SECOND PROPHET: The nonrecognition of my person as
unique of its kind.

FIRST PROPHET (*enters stage left*): So do I.

THE REGENT: And here's my answer: You can see for yourselves that your protests are unfounded. (*The two*
PROPHETS *stand face to face.*) Do you know each
other?

SECOND PROPHET: Strange! It's like looking in a mirror.

FIRST PROPHET: I also have the impression of looking in a
mirror.

SECOND PROPHET (*to* THE REGENT): If he's anything at all,
he's my reflection.

FIRST PROPHET: Funny reflection that says the same thing
as you.

THE REGENT: I'll settle this. (*Walks around first one, then
the other of the two* PROPHETS.)

SECOND PROPHET: Well?

FIRST PROPHET: What do you conclude?

THE REGENT: I can assure you that each of you is himself. I see you separately.

FIRST PROPHET (*to the* SECOND PROPHET): What shall we do?

SECOND PROPHET: We must come to an agreement.

FIRST PROPHET: Yes, that's the only solution.

They exit stage left. Enter GASPAR *from stage right.*

GASPAR: Must that woman sing?

THE REGENT: Why? Does it bother you?

GASPAR: My colleagues are complaining. They can't concentrate.

THE REGENT: I'm sorry, it can't be helped. We've got to keep the people busy. (*Hoots and catcalls from the square.* THE PRIMA DONNA *breaks off her aria and rushes into the hall. To* THE PRIMA DONNA.) What's up?

THE PRIMA DONNA: I can't work under these conditions.

THE REGENT: You're not happy with us?

THE PRIMA DONNA: I am an artist!

GASPAR (*glancing out at the square*): Utter confusion!

THE REGENT (*goes out on the balcony*): Looks like a riot to me.

GASPAR: Angrily, as though caught up in a giant maelstrom, the people are whirling about the enormous square. Look over there, under the lamppost.

THE REGENT: They're beating up the Bailiff!

GASPAR: The people, the people are rising.

THE REGENT: Rabble!

GASPAR: What are you going to do?

THE REGENT: We must hold their attention at all costs, give

them something interesting to look at, or they'll kill the old man. (*To* THE PRIMA DONNA.) I'm counting on you.

THE PRIMA DONNA: You wish me to sing more?

THE REGENT: Take your clothes off.

THE PRIMA DONNA: In front of gentlemen?

GASPAR: He's in the thick of the enemy.

THE REGENT: Quick! No time to lose. (*He pushes* THE PRIMA DONNA *out on the balcony and helps her to remove her dress. If necessary, she can wear flesh-colored tights simulating nudity. She attacks an aria. Shouts of enthusiasm from the square.*) It seems to be working. They're letting him go.

THE REGENT *and* GASPAR *leave the balcony,* GASPAR *reluctantly, turning his head to look at* THE PRIMA DONNA. *Enter on the left* MELCHIOR *and* BALTHAZAR.

MELCHIOR (*to* GASPAR): My dear colleague, what have you been doing? We've been looking all over for you, where were you?

GASPAR: Er... I've been helping to disperse a demonstration.

MELCHIOR: But we need you to help us draw our final conclusions.

THE REGENT: What are your conclusions?

MELCHIOR: So far, my dear Regent, we haven't got beyond the premises. (THE PRIMA DONNA *sings a* forte. MELCHIOR *stops his ears.*) Can't you get rid of her?

THE REGENT: Patience. Right now we need her.

MELCHIOR: After a rough computation of the probabilities,

we feel justified in presuming that this is the first case
of identical individuals in the world. For the first time
in history, two individuals have been born not only
physically but also biographically identical. The consequence of this biophysical and biographical identity is
that their intellectual and spiritual lives are also absolutely the same. This extraordinary coincidence has
been made possible by the enormousness of the world's
population today, which, I might mention in passing,
is still on the increase. However, what is most aston-
ishing from a scientific point of view is not the phenomenon itself but the social category in which it
occurred. If this had happened among peasants, sol-
diers, or football players, the mind might, in view of
the numerical magnitude of these population groups,
have been almost willing to accept it. But no. Fate has
decreed that this phenomenon should be embodied in
two identical specimens of the prophet-genius, an order of individuals who, as a general rule, make their
appearance only once in a thousand years. Here we ob-
serve the blind wastefulness of nature, its absence of rational planning. For so many centuries nothing, and
then suddenly two at once. What's more, identical.
And to make matters worse, this occurs at a time of
crisis when humanity is waiting for the one man who
can save it. And now its expectations are fulfilled, but
doubly. (THE PRIMA DONNA *sings a* forte.) Good God,
again!

THE REGENT: That's all very well, but as a man of action,
responsible for running this business, I can't do any-

thing with conclusions like that. The past is past. What concerns me is the future.

BALTHAZAR: That's the typical mistake practical politicians make. Effective action is possible only after a phenomenon has been analyzed in all its aspects. Before we can hope to take appropriate measures, we must determine the nature of the phenomenon.

THE REGENT: I look at it this way: we need one Prophet and we've got two. Which means that the second is not only superfluous, but in the way.

MELCHIOR: Yes, but only if you take the pragmatic view that the people are waiting for a single Prophet, an indivisible truth incarnated in one person, and so on. But why not look at it from the logical standpoint? Then it doesn't matter how many there are, because, being identical, they preach the same thing.

THE REGENT: The more the merrier. If one's as good as the other, there's no problem. We've only got to decide what to do with the other.

GASPAR: Put him in storage.

THE REGENT: Storage?

GASPAR: Keep him in reserve. Just in case. In case something happens to the first . . .

THE REGENT: Good idea.

BALTHAZAR: That might be risky. Experience teaches us that sooner or later mankind gets rid of its prophets by crucifixion. It's part of the program. What would we look like if, after mankind had done away with the first, the second turned up hale and hearty as if nothing had happened? Then he'd be first again, although he was second. What a deplorable effect, what a disappointment to the public! No more legend, no more irrevocable historical event. In short, scandal and confusion.

THE REGENT: We could wipe them both out when the time came, the acting Prophet and the one in storage.

BALTHAZAR: Can you be sure of perfect synchronization?

THE REGENT: No, I'm afraid I can't.

BALTHAZAR: You see!

MELCHIOR: Gentlemen, let's not beat about the bush. From all this it follows . . .

Pause.

THE REGENT: Go on.

MELCHIOR: I'd rather someone else completed my sentence.

BALTHAZAR: . . . that we should . . .

THE REGENT: . . . eliminate one of them right away. Why so squeamish? Was that your idea, Professor?

MELCHIOR: I didn't say it.

Silence.

THE REGENT: But which one?

MELCHIOR: From the standpoint of mankind, it makes no difference. (THE PRIMA DONNA *sings a* forte.) No, I can't stand it. I can't stand it! (*He stops his ears.*)

THE REGENT (*taking out a pocket watch on a chain*): We've got work to do. Where's the Bailiff? He ought to be here.

GASPAR: Perhaps he's hampered in his movements. Maybe they've injured him.

During this dialogue THE PRIMA DONNA *goes on singing, or rather, the recording of her voice goes on. The volume is turned up or down to fit in with the conversation which the singing should punctuate but not drown out.*

THE REGENT (*on the balcony*): Oh, the stinker! So that's what I pay him for!

BALTHAZAR: Who?

THE REGENT: The Bailiff. He's still down on the square.

MELCHIOR *and* BALTHAZAR *move a little to one side and talk in an undertone.*

GASPAR (*who has joined* THE REGENT *on the balcony*): He's down there with the crowd, listening to the concert.

THE REGENT: He's looking at us. (*He makes motions to attract* THE BAILIFF'*s attention.*) Pretending not to see us.

GASPAR: A stirring sight. The victim and his tormentors reconciled, listening to a siren.

THE REGENT: Listening, my foot!

GASPAR (*throwing his arms around* THE PRIMA DONNA): Madame, you're our new Orpheus.

THE REGENT: What's this? You too, Professor?

GASPAR: Art is my all.

THE REGENT (*leans down from the balcony*): No, he won't budge. There's only one solution.

He picks up THE PRIMA DONNA *bodily and throws her over the balustrade. Her song comes to an end like a sound tape when the current is cut off, slower and*

*slower, lower and lower-pitched until it dies out alto-
gether.* THE REGENT *raises his hands and shakes them
over his head like a victorious boxer receiving the ac-
clamations of the public.*

GASPAR (*swinging his left leg over the balustrade*): Wait for
me, Madame!

THE REGENT (*holding him back*): Professor! Don't! It's a
long drop.

GASPAR: That song. It bewitched me.

THE REGENT *and* GASPAR *return to the hall.*

MELCHIOR: At last you've switched her off.

THE REGENT: I was obliged to intervene in the interest of
my personnel. But now, with the people deprived of
entertainment, God knows what they'll do. (*He looks
at his watch.*) Five past eleven. It will take them half
an hour to collect their wits. That gives us a breathing
spell. After that we'll be in a fix. We've got to do
something quickly. (*Enter* THE BAILIFF *stage right,
limping.*) It's high time. Where's the ribbon? (THE
BAILIFF *weeps silently, discreetly wiping away his
tears.*) Come, come. Don't cry. I know it hurts.

THE BAILIFF: That's not the reason, boss.

THE REGENT: Then why are you sobbing?

THE BAILIFF: She sang so beautifully!

THE REGENT: Shame on you! At your age!

THE BAILIFF: My age? I'm younger than you, boss.

THE REGENT: Forget it. Where's the ribbon?

THE BAILIFF: They wouldn't give it to me, boss.

THE REGENT: I told you to use force.

THE BAILIFF: I did, boss.

THE REGENT: Well?

THE BAILIFF: They didn't understand.

THE REGENT (*to the* THREE WISE MEN): Hear that? The situation is even more serious than I thought. They refuse to restore the power. This is anarchy!

THE BAILIFF: Do you still need me, Mr. Regent?

THE REGENT: More than ever. You've done your military service, I presume?

THE BAILIFF: Yes, sir. In the cavalry.

THE REGENT: Excellent. Then you know how to cut off heads.

THE BAILIFF: Not really, boss. I was a cook.

THE REGENT: Same thing. You chopped the heads off chickens.

THE BAILIFF: I didn't care for that at all.

THE REGENT: Pay close attention. Go up to the attic and get an ax. Dust it off and sharpen it up a bit and bring it here to me. (THE BAILIFF *grimaces.*) What is the meaning of that face?

THE BAILIFF: I might cut myself. . . .

THE REGENT: Oh no! You can cut yourself tomorrow if you feel like it. Right now I want you in good health.

THE BAILIFF: A kind thought. Same to you, boss.

He exits left. The THREE WISE MEN *whisper together, then they, too, head for the door stage right.*

THE REGENT: Where are you going?

MELCHIOR: We wish to wash our hands.

THE REGENT: Now?

GASPAR: While the opportunity offers . . .

THE REGENT: Are you deserting? (*Pause.*) Not a bad idea, come to think of it. Let's all go and wash our hands.

They all exit stage right. The two PROPHETS *enter stage left.*

FIRST PROPHET: In our garden there were raspberries. If I'm not mistaken there were forty thousand eight hundred and thirty-two of them.

SECOND PROPHET: Amazing. In our garden, too.

FIRST PROPHET: How many?

SECOND PROPHET: Exactly the same number—if I'm not mistaken.

FIRST PROPHET: Astounding—this resemblance in every detail.

SECOND PROPHET: My uncle was crazy about salad.

FIRST PROPHET: Plain!

SECOND PROPHET: No, with Russian dressing.

FIRST PROPHET: I meant it's plain that he liked it with Russian dressing.

SECOND PROPHET: Too bad. I thought we'd found a difference.

FIRST PROPHET: Let's not kid ourselves. We're identical.

Pause.

SECOND PROPHET: Does your back ache, too?

FIRST PROPHET: Stop! It's no use.

SECOND PROPHET: I only thought . . .

FIRST PROPHET: I understand, but we've got to face the facts.

SECOND PROPHET: All the same I'd like an answer.

FIRST PROPHET: It aches! It aches! It aches!

SECOND PROPHET: Yes, of course.

FIRST PROPHET: What did you think? That it didn't ache? If you must know, it aches something awful. Satisfied? You're beginning to get on my nerves!

SECOND PROPHET (*raising his voice*): You're getting on my nerves, too!

Pause. Both burst out laughing.

FIRST PROPHET: You see, we each get on the other's nerves. Let's cut this out, we're not getting anywhere.

SECOND PROPHET: Now what's going to happen?

FIRST PROPHET: I was told to wait.

SECOND PROPHET: Needless to say, I too was told to ...

FIRST PROPHET: I wonder what they're plotting.

SECOND PROPHET: So do——

The FIRST PROPHET claps his hand over his mouth.

FIRST PROPHET: I'm getting fed up.

SECOND PROPHET: So am—— Oh, excuse me.

FIRST PROPHET: Never mind. If you know it, I know it.

SECOND PROPHET: Listen. I've got an idea—you too?

FIRST PROPHET: I can imagine ... but go ahead.

SECOND PROPHET: Since we have the same message for all mankind, what difference does it make which one of us delivers it?

FIRST PROPHET: What are you getting at?

SECOND PROPHET: Go on. It's your turn.

Pause.

FIRST PROPHET: I fully agree with you.

SECOND PROPHET: Well?

Pause. They look at each other. Enter stage right THE REGENT *wiping his hands on a towel, followed by the* THREE WISE MEN *who shake their wet hands or wipe them discreetly on their robes.*

BALTHAZAR: Could I have the towel, Regent?

THE REGENT: Here. (*He hands* BALTHAZAR *the towel. To the two* PROPHETS.) Ah, our guests.

FIRST PROPHET: Who are these gentlemen?

THE REGENT: Ah yes, forgive me. You haven't met. Professor Balthazar . . .

BALTHAZAR (*hastily finishes drying his hands and passes the towel to* MELCHIOR): Glad to meet you. (*He shakes hands with the* PROPHETS.)

THE REGENT: Professor Melchior . . .

MELCHIOR *nervously finishes drying his hands and passes the towel behind his back to* GASPAR *who, in addition to his hands, dries his ears.*

MELCHIOR: Delighted . . . (*He shakes hands with the* PROPHETS.)

THE REGENT: Assistant Professor Gaspar . . .

GASPAR *clumsily stuffs the towel into his pocket.*

GASPAR: Pleased to . . .

FIRST PROPHET (*aside to* SECOND PROPHET): Have you noticed how friendly they are all of a sudden?

SECOND PROPHET: Strange, isn't it? Oh, well.

> *The* THREE WISE MEN *clear their throats as usual when they do not know who is going to start the conversation.*

THE REGENT (*to the* PROPHETS): I'm happy to see you're on good terms.

FIRST PROPHET: We've come to an agreement.

THE REGENT: And what have you agreed about, may I ask?

FIRST PROPHET: Since neither one of us is equipped to proclaim the beginning of the new era, my friend here has suggested——

SECOND PROPHET (*interrupting*): What?

FIRST PROPHET: —that I should do so.

THE REGENT: Splendid. That's what I call cooperation. (*Aside to the* THREE WISE MEN.) The choice will be less difficult than I feared. (*To the* SECOND PROPHET.) Is this true?

SECOND PROPHET: Absolutely . . .

FIRST PROPHET: Thank you, my friend.

THE REGENT (*to* FIRST PROPHET): Congratulations! (*Aside to the* THREE WISE MEN.) That does make things easier. (*To the* FIRST PROPHET.) Kindly step out on the balcony.

SECOND PROPHET: Except for one detail. I didn't make that suggestion to him. He made it to me.

THE REGENT: One of you must be joking.

SECOND PROPHET: Not I.

FIRST PROPHET: Think back. You began.

SECOND PROPHET: But you finished.

THE REGENT: Let's not split hairs. The public wants—how shall I put it—a clear-cut answer.

MELCHIOR: Gentlemen, permit me to say a few words. The idea as such is not bad. Since you both have the same thing to say, personal considerations are immaterial. Nay more, it is noble to cede one's place. Since he who chooses to withdraw can rest assured that his idea—since it coincides with his friend's idea—will not incur the slightest loss, his action will gratify him for two reasons: one, because he has stepped aside, so demonstrating his generosity, and two, because nothing has been lost.

BALTHAZAR: Exactly.

GASPAR: It's self-evident.

FIRST PROPHET: Hear that?

SECOND PROPHET: Hear that?

THE REGENT: Professor Melchior is right. I personally envy the one of you who stands aside. So who will it be? (A *long pause.* THE REGENT *takes out his watch and taps it impatiently with his finger.*) Gentlemen, there's no time to lose.

An ax falls in the middle of the stage. It is not a stage prop but a real ax, large and heavy, with a broad blade.

FIRST PROPHET: Something dropped.

THE REGENT: Mere illusion.

SECOND PROPHET: Sounded like iron.

THE REGENT: Not at all.

THE BAILIFF (*leaning down from the grid*): Mr. Regent!

THE REGENT: It's only my Bailiff. Now what?

132 / Slawomir Mrozek

THE BAILIFF: Have you got it?

THE REGENT: What are you talking about?

THE BAILIFF: The damn thing slipped out of my hands.

THE REGENT: What are you doing up there?

THE BAILIFF: But you told me——

THE REGENT: Come down here this minute and don't talk so much!

THE BAILIFF: Yes, Mr. Regent. (*He disappears.*)

THE REGENT: Let's get back to our problem. (*To the* SECOND PROPHET.) You don't wish to be noble?

SECOND PROPHET: Me? There's been a misunderstanding. Let me anticipate the reproach I can read in your eyes. If I am disinclined to give way to my friend, it doesn't mean that I despise a noble action. But you could also say that the desire to distinguish oneself by noble actions is a sign of pride and that true virtue consists in humbly declining such an opportunity to demonstrate nobility of soul. If I decline to stand aside, it's not because I don't want to.

THE REGENT: Then what the hell is your reason?

SECOND PROPHET: Because I can't.

THE REGENT: Why can't you?

SECOND PROPHET: By standing aside, I should be showing greater nobility of spirit than my friend, as Professor Melchior has just pointed out. In other words, I should be superior to my double. That's the crux of the matter. I can't allow a man who is inferior to me to become the Prophet, because that would be a crime against mankind, which expects a Prophet of the highest order.

THE REGENT: Well, if you don't want——

SECOND PROPHET: I beg your pardon, I can't.

THE REGENT: Comes to the same thing. (*To the* FIRST PROPHET.) Then *you* stand aside.

FIRST PROPHET: Very well.

THE REGENT: Bravo!

SECOND PROPHET: I must be dreaming.

MELCHIOR: That's what I call a decision!

BALTHAZAR: Come to my arms!

GASPAR: Whew, what a relief!

FIRST PROPHET: I'm only too glad to oblige you, gentlemen, and to please the people——

THE REGENT: Good. That settles it. (*To the* SECOND PROPHET.) Now you, you go out on the balcony. (*To the* FIRST PROPHET.) And you— (*He claps his hands.*) Bailiff! Hey, Bailiff! Now where has he gone?

FIRST PROPHET: —and to give an example of humility and renunciation——

MELCHIOR: Yes, yes, it's a fine thing.

FIRST PROPHET: But unfortunately——

THE REGENT: Unfortunately? You're not going to tell me *you* can't——

FIRST PROPHET: Not at all. I can . . .

THE REGENT: Thank God. (*He pats the* FIRST PROPHET *on the back.*) You had me scared.

FIRST PROPHET: It's you who can't.

THE REGENT: What!

FIRST PROPHET: You can't accept my resignation. In view of what my friend here has said, you can't permit such a scandal, you can't allow the nobler and more disinterested of us to stand aside. And who is the nobler? The one who voluntarily stands aside.

BALTHAZAR: But the one who stands aside can't become the Prophet if he stands aside.

FIRST PROPHET: That's the whole trouble. And that's why you won't accept my resignation. I can't help it.

THE REGENT (*to the* THREE WISE MEN): Well, what do you say? Can we or can't we?

FIRST PROPHET: Would you want to make the inferior man Prophet and send the better man into retirement? No, gentlemen, I can't believe that. That would be cheating mankind.

GASPAR: An inextricable tangle!

THE REGENT (*to* MELCHIOR): Say something, Professor. Prove that he's wrong, that both of them are wrong. (*Aside to* MELCHIOR.) Save us!

MELCHIOR: Hmm ... (*Taking a professorial tone.*) Though fully appreciating your misgivings, gentlemen ... yes, fully appreciating ... notwithstanding ...

THE REGENT: That's it, notwithstanding. Pay close attention, gentlemen. (*Aside to* MELCHIOR.) Stop hemming and hawing.

MELCHIOR (*aside*): Don't hurry me. (*Aloud.*) While understanding your motives in declining to stand aside ... (*To* THE REGENT.) Am I making myself clear?

THE REGENT: Yes, yes. Very clear.

MELCHIOR: In spite of everything, or rather, for that very reason ... (*He ponders.*) Yes, in spite of everything ... (*He ponders.*) No, for that very reason ... Or perhaps ... (*He ponders.*) No, it's in spite of ...

THE REGENT: Make up your mind.

MELCHIOR: I'm sorry. I've lost the thread.

THE REGENT: You're tired, Professor. (*To* MELCHIOR, *aside.*) Fine work!

MELCHIOR: What do you want of me? I'm only a simple professor, he's a genius. (*Grumbling of the crowd from the square.* THE REGENT *looks at his watch.*) Half-past eleven. (*To the* PROPHETS, *sharply.*) Now leave us alone. From this moment on you will do as we say. Since you refuse to settle this peacefully between yourselves, you will have to accept our decision. We will choose the Prophet.

The PROPHETS *exit stage left.*

THE BAILIFF (*runs in breathless from the right*): Boss!

THE REGENT: Ah, there you are! Who told you to throw that thing down? You might have killed somebody.

Explosions from the square.

THE BAILIFF: Boss, they're getting bored. They're only smashing street lights now but God knows what they'll think of next. (*Explosions.*) Listen to that! They're frustrated. They're drinking whiskey.

GASPAR: I wouldn't mind a little myself. I don't feel so good.

THE REGENT: Haven't they got any Jews? Or early Christians? Or Armenians? Or blacks? Some such thing. Why does it have to be street lights?

THE BAILIFF: We had a few, but they're gone.

BALTHAZAR: Give them games to play. The people have always liked games. *Panem et circenses!* Wild animals. Gladiators . . .

THE REGENT: Where am I going to find gladiators?

BALTHAZAR: That's your business.

THE REGENT: We can give it a try. (*To* THE BAILIFF.) Go get a lion and wrestle with it on the square.

THE BAILIFF: A lion?

THE REGENT: A tiger if you prefer.

THE BAILIFF: Wouldn't an alley cat do the trick?

THE REGENT: A lion, I said.

THE BAILIFF: Okay, boss. (*He exits stage left.*)

THE REGENT: Quick now. Which one do we get rid of?

GASPAR: I'm feeling a little sick to my stomach.

MELCHIOR: Wouldn't it be better to——

THE REGENT: We haven't got all day.

MELCHIOR: —exterminate mankind. From the standpoint of morality it would be much better than having one of those poor unfortunates on our consciences.

BALTHAZAR: I beg to disagree. If mankind perished, there wouldn't be any morality left. Furthermore, my dear colleague, there wouldn't be anyone left to admire your brilliance.

From the square the roars of a lion and the cries of the frenzied crowd are heard.

GASPAR: I hate them! Why can't they eliminate each other? Why do I have to do it for them? It gives me a belly-ache. It isn't human of them, it isn't right, it isn't . . . I'll . . . I'll . . . (*Takes the ax from the floor and runs stage left.*)

THE REGENT (*bars his way*): Where are you going?

GASPAR (*brandishing the ax*): I'm going to punish them.

THE REGENT: Have you gone mad? We only have to get rid of one. We can't touch a hair of the other's head. Calm down. Stop your hysterics. Give me that.

GASPAR: It's my nerves.

He gives THE REGENT *the ax and goes off to one side.*

BALTHAZAR: If we give them a chance, maybe one of them will find a way of liquidating the other. That way we wouldn't have to do anything.

GASPAR: God willing!

THE REGENT: All right. Why not? It's our last hope. (*He drives the ax into the floor in the middle of the stage.*) We'll go hide on the balcony. (*One by one the* THREE WISE MEN *go out on the balcony and hide.* THE REGENT *claps his hands.*) Come in! Come in!

He also runs to the balcony and hides. The two PROPHETS *enter from stage left.*

FIRST PROPHET: That's funny, there's no one here.

SECOND PROPHET: I distinctly heard them calling us. They must have made their choice.

The lion roars. Both PROPHETS *slowly approach the ax. They stop a few steps away from it, cross their hands behind their backs, and go back slowly toward stage left as though taking a walk.*

FIRST PROPHET: Do you think it's you they've picked?

SECOND PROPHET: Why do you ask?

FIRST PROPHET: No reason.

Pause. The lion roars. They go to the stage left end of the stage and, still together, return to the center.

SECOND PROPHET: Are you under the impression——
FIRST PROPHET: What impression?
SECOND PROPHET: That they've chosen you——
FIRST PROPHET: Why do you ask?
SECOND PROPHET: Because I'd like to know.

They step in front of the ax. The lion roars. Slowly they circle round the ax, one behind the other, remaining at an equal distance from the center. The SECOND PROPHET is in the lead.

FIRST PROPHET: Do you think . . . it's me?
SECOND PROPHET: No.
FIRST PROPHET: You?
SECOND PROPHET: No.

Pause. The lion roars.

FIRST PROPHET: Not me?
SECOND PROPHET: No.
FIRST PROPHET: Aha, then you?
SECOND PROPHET: Not me.
FIRST PROPHET: Not you?
SECOND PROPHET: No.
FIRST PROPHET: What do you mean, no?
SECOND PROPHET: Don't you agree?

Pause. Having completed exactly a circuit and a half, they go off again side by side, this time to stage right.

FIRST PROPHET: You answer first.

SECOND PROPHET: Why me?

FIRST PROPHET: Because I asked first.

SECOND PROPHET: What do you think my answer will be?

FIRST PROPHET: What do you think I think your answer will be?

SECOND PROPHET: I'll tell you what I think when you've told me what you think I think . . .

They stop.

FIRST PROPHET: You?

SECOND PROPHET: Me.

FIRST PROPHET: Me?

SECOND PROPHET: You.

Pause. A shattering roar from the lion and the crowd. The PROPHETS turn around, both at the same time, and start running, holding their hands out toward the ax. Enter from stage left THE BAILIFF wearing a gilded fireman's helmet. Seeing him, the PROPHETS, already bending over to seize the ax, stop still and straighten up, making each movement simultaneously. Suddenly the roaring of the lion and the crowd stops.

THE BAILIFF: Mr. Regent . . . (*He looks around.*) Isn't the boss here?

FIRST PROPHET: We haven't seen him.

THE BAILIFF: He's lucky. When he feels like it he's here, when he doesn't, he's not. Not like a poor bailiff who always has to be on the spot.

THE REGENT (*coming from the balcony*): Do I hear complaints? What's wrong?

THE BAILIFF: Here's the boss.

THE REGENT: I didn't ask you who was here. I asked you what was wrong. What are you doing here, why aren't you in there fighting?

THE BAILIFF: Trouble, boss.

THE REGENT: You're tired?

THE BAILIFF: Not me—the lion.

THE REGENT: The lion?

THE BAILIFF: He's not feeling well.

THE REGENT: What's the matter with him?

THE BAILIFF: He's feeling faint.

THE REGENT: A lion? The king of beasts? Nonsense. You're a lazy good-for-nothing, that's what you are. I don't accept such explanations.

THE BAILIFF: But he really did seem faint. Or maybe even worse.

THE REGENT: What!

THE BAILIFF: The crowd smothered him. They trampled the poor fellow to death.

THE REGENT: A lion?

THE BAILIFF: You just can't imagine, boss, what a crush there is in the world today. That crowd! What do you know about crowds? You've got your official space, your official air, your private carriage, and your apartment in the palace. A lion hasn't got all that.

THE REGENT: May his memory be honored! We'll give him the Order of the Golden Lamb, posthumously. Wait here.

THE BAILIFF: Where is he going to put it? They've made hash out of him. Poor old fellow! He was a good little lion. (*He fans himself with his helmet.*)

THE REGENT (*to the* PROPHETS): Kindly leave us. (*The* PROPHETS *start to the right of the stage.*) No. One to the right, one to the left.

SECOND PROPHET: Which one to the left?

THE REGENT: It doesn't matter. (*The* SECOND PROPHET *goes out left, the* FIRST PROPHET *right. The* THREE WISE MEN, *very much excited, enter from the balcony.* GASPAR *has taken the towel out of his pocket and is mopping his forehead.*) Did you see that . . . ?

MELCHIOR: Yes. Well, it didn't come off.

BALTHAZAR: It almost did, though. If it hadn't been for this imbecile—— (*To* THE BAILIFF.) Why the devil did you have to butt in?

THE BAILIFF: The lion—*kaputt* . . .

THE REGENT: Leave him alone. He only did his duty.

BALTHAZAR: It's stifling. . . . There's going to be a storm. (*He loosens the collar of his robe.*)

MELCHIOR: The people are strangely calm.

THE REGENT: I don't trust this weather. Or the people, either. It's the quiet before the storm. (*Pause.* THE REGENT *goes over to* THE BAILIFF.) Have you ever played pretty penny?

THE BAILIFF: I used to, when I was a kid.

THE REGENT: Good.

THE BAILIFF: But I don't play anymore. I'm too old for that stuff. A grown man has other things to worry about.

THE REGENT (*waggishly*): Even so, we could give it a try. . . . How about it?

THE BAILIFF: You and me, boss?

THE REGENT: Why not?

THE BAILIFF: Aw, you're joking, boss. We're adults. At least I am. I don't know about you.

THE REGENT: What difference does that make? In every grown man's bosom there lurks a child. Don't you ever feel a little rascal stirring inside you?

THE BAILIFF (*laughing with embarrassment*): Hee-hee-hee!

THE REGENT: A wee little tot?

THE BAILIFF: You're in pretty good humor today, boss. I only hope it lasts.

THE REGENT: All right, let's play. I too like to go back to the age of innocence. (*He takes a piece of candy wrapped in silver paper from his pocket, removes the paper and opens his mouth.*) Pop! (*He tosses the candy into his mouth. Though still embarrassed,* THE BAILIFF *laughs whole-heartedly.*) Now, watch closely! (THE REGENT *rolls the silver paper into a ball, takes the ball between two fingers, shows it to each of those present in turn, then turns toward* THE BAILIFF.) Take a penny, hold it tight,

Where's the penny, left or right?

THE BAILIFF: Eeny, meeny, miny, mo. (*He points to* THE REGENT's *left hand.*)

THE REGENT: Left hand! (*He opens his hand and holds the paper out.*)

THE BAILIFF: There it is!

The THREE WISE MEN *applaud.*

THE REGENT: You win! Lucky man!

THE BAILIFF (*proud of his success*): Yes, I guess I am lucky.

He puts the ball of paper in his pocket. All laugh. The gay, relaxed atmosphere of a group playing parlor games.

THE REGENT: See what fun it is? Sometimes we need a little distraction.

THE BAILIFF: I'd like ...

THE REGENT: Yes?

THE BAILIFF: Since you're so playful today, boss, so kind, I mean, such a pal, if you don't mind my saying so ...

THE REGENT (*slapping him on the back*): Go on. Don't be afraid. Speak as you would to a friend.

THE BAILIFF: I'd like to play some more.

All laugh.

THE REGENT: Full of beans, aren't you? What would you like to play? Pretty penny again?

THE BAILIFF: Sure, why not?

THE REGENT: No, let's play something else. Let's see ... (*He takes* THE BAILIFF *by the arm, they walk back and forth.*) Hm ... say, do you know how to play hop-skip-jump?

THE BAILIFF: Hop-skip-jump?

THE REGENT: Hop-skip-jump.

THE BAILIFF: No. How does it go?

THE REGENT: Well, you take something sharp——

THE BAILIFF: Scissors?

THE REGENT: Hm ... that depends. Maybe something a little bigger ... Ah! (*He picks up the ax.*) This is just what we need. Take it. (*He puts the ax into* THE BAILIFF'*s hand.*)

THE BAILIFF (*suddenly suspicious*): Is it complicated?

THE REGENT: Easy as pie. You hop aside and chop the head off. A child can do it.

THE BAILIFF: That's hop-skip-jump?

THE REGENT (*without assurance*): Yes. Hop-skip-jump.

THE BAILIFF (*puts the ax down on the floor*): No, thank you.

THE REGENT: You don't want to play anymore?

THE BAILIFF: I'd rather go to a whorehouse.

THE REGENT (*suddenly severe and commanding*): We've had enough of your jokes! Where do you think you are? Kindergarten?

THE BAILIFF: You started it, boss. . . .

THE REGENT: Be quiet! An old man like you horsing around like a little snotnose!

THE BAILIFF: It wasn't my idea.

THE REGENT: This is a place of business! A serious institution. And don't forget it! What do you think I am? Your nurse?

THE BAILIFF: I never said that, boss. I'm not blind.

THE REGENT: You're my subordinate and it's your duty to carry out my orders! Now you will go and chop. (THE BAILIFF *is silent.*) Understand?

MELCHIOR: I think we'd better stretch our legs.

BALTHAZAR: Yes, let's go out on the balcony.

GASPAR: I need some fresh air.

The THREE WISE MEN *go out on the balcony.*

THE REGENT (*to* THE BAILIFF, *gently*): Listen to me. No one is asking you to act like a ruffian. This is an affair of state, a service we must render humanity. That's what we're here for. (THE BAILIFF *is silent*.) Have you got instincts?

THE BAILIFF: Instincts?

THE REGENT: Let's put it this way. Do you ever feel like doing something people get put in jail for?

THE BAILIFF: Me, boss?

THE REGENT: Admit it, just between you and me.

THE BAILIFF: Well, maybe . . . sometimes . . .

THE REGENT: What, for instance?

THE BAILIFF: Sometimes when I look at you, boss, I want to . . . to . . . (*He makes the gesture of breaking something in two.*) Like this . . . (*He presses both fists against his chest.*) And then like this . . . (*He thrusts his fists violently forward.*)

THE REGENT: Me? Why me?

THE BAILIFF: You know. For old times' sake.

THE REGENT: That's not nice.

THE BAILIFF: But I'd never do it . . . I wouldn't dare. It's all in my imagination. Why am I telling you this anyway?

THE REGENT: You see. We all have our instincts. It's very sad. But remember, we mustn't let them carry us away.

THE BAILIFF: Heaven forbid!

THE REGENT: I'm glad you feel that way about it. But now listen to me. What you have to do now—will you do it gladly or reluctantly?

THE BAILIFF: Chopping off the head, you mean?

THE REGENT: Answer me.

THE BAILIFF (*reflecting*): Not gladly.

THE REGENT: Excellent. I see you're a morally healthy individual. But why won't you do it gladly?

THE BAILIFF: Because—somehow—my conscience——

THE REGENT: Splendid, splendid. Then it's all right for you to do it.

THE BAILIFF: You mean in spite of my conscience?

THE REGENT: If you were only a common murderer wanting to satisfy your instincts, I'd never ask you to do such a thing. On the contrary, I'd have you thrown in jail. But you're morally sound. And because you're morally sound I can entrust you with this painful task. A head has to be cut off. Not for anybody's private pleasure but for the public welfare. Consequently, the man who does it must do it *in spite* of his conscience. Otherwise it would be a private pleasure, not a heroic action. You will chop, your conscience will torment you, and everything will be in order. It's the conflict that counts.

THE BAILIFF: Then I have to kill?

THE REGENT: General considerations call for a general terminology, private considerations for a private terminology. Since you are going to act in the name of a general consideration and not for private purposes, the word you have just used is out of place. Not "kill." Eliminate.

THE BAILIFF: Doesn't it mean the same thing?

THE REGENT: Yes and no. I've just explained the difference, haven't I? Eliminate. Or better still, liquidate.

THE BAILIFF (*tries to repeat it*): Li-, li- . . .

THE REGENT: Li-qui-date.

THE BAILIFF: That's a hard word. Is it foreign?

THE REGENT: Not at all. It's absolutely indigenous. Native. National.

THE BAILIFF: I'm glad to hear that. I'm a patriot. (*He puts on the helmet, takes the ax in both hands. A few steps to the right, a few steps to the left.*) But which one?

THE REGENT: You've already chosen. The one on the left. (THE BAILIFF *moves to stage left.*) And don't forget— without enthusiasm.

THE BAILIFF: Don't worry. (*He exits stage left.*)

THE REGENT (*exhausted, he goes toward the balcony*): That's that. (*He mops his brow.*)

Enter the THREE WISE MEN. GASPAR *is leaning on* BALTHAZAR's *arm.*

MELCHIOR: I wish it were all over.

THE REGENT: You're not satisfied? I'd have liked to see you try to soften him up. Here I knock myself out for you people and all I get is complaints.

MELCHIOR: Not at all. We fully appreciate . . .

THE REGENT: It's all very well to be a Wise Man, but when the going gets rough, it's up to the Regent . . .

GASPAR (*in a feeble voice*): Is it all over?

THE REGENT: What's wrong with him?

BALTHAZAR: He's not feeling very well.

THE REGENT: Hmm, a sensitive soul. What about me? Haven't I got a soul? Is a statesman an animal? You think I enjoy this? Nobody asks me how I feel.

MELCHIOR: We're all human. In this heavy hour permit me to express my profound sympathy to us all. In

a moment, fortunately, our labors will have borne
fruit. We shall be able to proclaim the Prophet. The
one Prophet. (*A pause. To* BALTHAZAR.) You seem
thoughtful, Professor.

BALTHAZAR: I'm wondering if we washed our hands enough.

MELCHIOR: Did you use the soap?

BALTHAZAR: It was foul.

THE REGENT (*taking out his watch*): Why is it taking so
long?

Pause. They stand motionless. THE REGENT *looks at his
watch. From stage left are heard a muffled blow, then
the sound of something striking the floor.* THE REGENT
puts his watch back in his vest pocket.

MELCHIOR: Hallelujah!

GASPAR *sinks into* BALTHAZAR's *arms.*

BALTHAZAR: He's fainted!

MELCHIOR: Whew. It's over. All's well that ends well. I'll
get him. (*He starts to stage right.*)

THE REGENT: Wait. We've got to be sure.

All turn toward the door stage left. THE BAILIFF *runs in
wearing the helmet and brandishing the ax. In his
right hand a replica of the* SECOND PROPHET's *head. Because this head was a mask to begin with, which in turn
was a reproduction or stylized replica of a classical
sculpture, there will be no gruesome effect.*

THE BAILIFF: Next! (*He runs to stage right.*)

THE REGENT (*barring his way*): Stop, stop! I fobid you!

THE BAILIFF: Why?

THE REGENT: Because the other one is innocent.

THE BAILIFF: Give me the innocent one! (*He runs to stage right.*)

THE REGENT (*barring his way*): Don't you dare!

THE BAILIFF (*stopping still*): No next?

THE REGENT: No.

THE BAILIFF: Too bad.

THE REGENT: Have you gone crazy?

THE BAILIFF: I'm getting to like this work.

THE REGENT: It was understood that you would do it reluctantly.

THE BAILIFF: They always say that.

THE REGENT: In spite of your conscience!

THE BAILIFF (*pleading*): Couldn't you find me something else, boss . . . ?

THE REGENT: No, that's all there is.

THE BAILIFF: I was just getting warmed up.

THE REGENT: The orgy's over! Give me that and go and repent of your action.

THE BAILIFF: Aw, you're always like that, boss.

MELCHIOR: Bloodthirsty monster!

THE BAILIFF *gives the* SECOND PROPHET's *head to* THE REGENT *and goes into a corner.*

THE REGENT: No, there's no room for doubt. (*He shows the head to the* THREE WISE MEN.) Here is the proof.

MELCHIOR: Can we look? (*He examines the head.*) Yes, that's it.

THE REGENT: Hold it a second . . . (*He gives* MELCHIOR *the head.*) I'll go get the other prophet. (*He goes toward stage right.*) Meanwhile, gentlemen, tidy yourselves up a bit. From this moment on he will be our only master. He is entitled to glory and respect. We shall welcome him with the highest honors. I believe that's what you gentlemen came for.

The THREE WISE MEN *put their clothes in order.* BALTHAZAR *pets* GASPAR's *cheeks and he staggers to his feet.* THE REGENT *pulls his jacket into place, straightens his shirt front. He goes out left with elastic but solemn step. Pause.* THE BAILIFF *has sat down on the floor upstage right and has started hacking at the floor with the ax. Immersed in his occupation, he pays no attention to the others. Atmosphere of expectancy. Backstage a brief but violent gust of wind. Steps are heard.*

BALTHAZAR: They're coming!

MELCHIOR, *suddenly realizing that he is still holding the* SECOND PROPHET's *head, is seized with panic, like someone who does not know how to get rid of a compromising object. Finally he puts it on the floor and freezes into a solemn pose.* THE REGENT *enters from the left. He walks slowly, dragging his feet, bowed and dejected, his hands folded behind his back. He stops near the door.*

BALTHAZAR: Where is he?
MELCHIOR: Is he coming?

THE BAILIFF *stops hacking at the floor, but does not stand up. He gapes at the others.* THE REGENT *stands motionless and silent.*

BALTHAZAR: Has something happened?

MELCHIOR: Why doesn't he come? (*Pause.*) Regent, what's wrong?

THE REGENT (*hoarsely, without raising his head*): A disaster, gentlemen.

MELCHIOR: Has he escaped?

THE REGENT: When I entered the vast hall where our master was waiting, our hope, our holy . . . our one and only . . . beloved teacher . . . (*His voice breaks.*)

THE BAILIFF *stands up, comes closer and listens.*

MELCHIOR: Go on.

THE REGENT: I opened the door.

BALTHAZAR: I should think so. How else would you get in?

MELCHIOR: To the point!

THE REGENT: There was a window in the hall.

BALTHAZAR: Nothing new about that either. (*To* MELCHIOR.) He's raving.

THE REGENT: When I went in, the master arose with a gentle smile. There he stood, exalted and serene, noble and beautiful. (*Erupting.*) Why didn't he lie down? At that moment . . .

MELCHIOR: I have a dark foreboding.

THE REGENT: A violent wind came up . . .

MELCHIOR (*covering his face with his robe*): Say no more!

THE REGENT: . . . and blew off his head . . . Here it is.

He raises his arm and shows the FIRST PROPHET's *head, which he had been hiding behind his back.*

BALTHAZAR: Our beloved master!

MELCHIOR: Our Prophet!

THE REGENT: Dead.

THE BAILIFF: And they wouldn't let *me*!

> *A flash of lightning, thunder in the distance. The light dims.*

GASPAR (*suddenly bursts out laughing*): No, this is too much. It's absurd . . . (*He goes off to one side, still laughing.*)

THE REGENT: Now what's the matter with him?

MELCHIOR: Is this a time to laugh? When the Messiah has died! Blasphemy!

BALTHAZAR: Gaspar, calm yourself!

GASPAR: I refuse to believe it, do you hear? I refuse!

MELCHIOR: How can you refuse, Professor . . . (*He points to the head that* THE REGENT *is holding.*) Doesn't that convince you? We must face the facts.

GASPAR (*picking up the* SECOND PROPHET's *head from the floor*): Greetings, little head.

MELCHIOR: He's lost his mind.

BALTHAZAR: It must be the shock.

GASPAR (*wagging a threatening forefinger at the* SECOND PROPHET's *head*): Oh, oh, is that nice? No arms, no legs . . . What a naughty Prophet!

MELCHIOR: Permit me to call to your attention the fact that that is not the Prophet. The Regent is holding the Prophet.

GASPAR: Oh, I beg your pardon. (*To the* SECOND PROPHET's *head that he is still holding.*) Don't be afraid. I know what's what. I won't let them put anything over on you. (*He approaches* THE REGENT.) Can I have the Prophet?

THE REGENT (*hiding the* FIRST PROPHET'*s head behind his back*): What do you want him for?

GASPAR: He's my friend. I want to play with him.

BALTHAZAR: Gaspar!

GASPAR (*stamping his foot like a spoiled child*): I want the Pro-o-phet! (*He sobs.*)

THE REGENT (*hesitating*): Should I?

MELCHIOR: I think you'd better give in.

BALTHAZAR: Don't cross him. He seems to have lost his wits.

GASPAR (*whining*): The Pro-o-phet . . .

THE REGENT: All right . . . Here, but don't lose him. (*He gives* GASPAR *the* FIRST PROPHET'*s head. To* MELCHIOR *and* BALTHAZAR.) Anyway he's no use to us anymore.

GASPAR: No, sir. (*He moves off hastily like a child who is afraid the grown-ups will change their minds and take his toy away.* THE BAILIFF *follows him, looking curiously over his shoulder.* GASPAR *stops, facing the audience.* THE BAILIFF *behind him.* GASPAR *addresses the* FIRST PROPHET'*s head which he is holding in his left hand.*) They didn't want to give you to me. But what have I got a head for? Now, now. No offense, I meant my own. (*He taps his forehead insofar as this is technically possible.*) You fellows will make out all right, I promise you. Are you happy, little ball? (*To the* SECOND PROPHET'*s head in his right hand.*) And you, little apple? (*Pause.*) What's that? (*He presses his ear to the* SECOND PROPHET'*s head, listens, laughs, nods his*

head.) Yes, yes, you're right. I'll tell him. (*He whispers
in the* FIRST PROPHET'*s ear*.)

THE BAILIFF (*standing on tiptoe to see over* GASPAR'*s shoulder*): Can I look?

GASPAR: A stranger! We must flee! (*Pressing both heads to
his chest he runs into a corner and turns his face to
the wall*.)

THE BAILIFF: He's not very obliging.

BALTHAZAR: First a murder, then an accident, and now
madness. I can't stand it.

THE REGENT: I protest against the word "murder." It was
a liquidation.

BALTHAZAR: Anyway, it stinks.

MELCHIOR: Gentlemen, not in front of the personnel.

THE REGENT: If that's how you feel about it, let me point
out that you are at least as responsible as I am.

THE BAILIFF *approaches and follows the scene with
interest*.

BALTHAZAR: Me?

THE REGENT: Yes, you!

BALTHAZAR *and* THE REGENT *are face to face in threatening attitudes, their bellies almost touching*.

THE BAILIFF: Sock him!

THE REGENT: Who told you to butt in?

THE BAILIFF: I was talking to myself. Something I remem-
bered. (*He moves off*.) Nobody wants to talk to me
anymore.

MELCHIOR: Gentlemen, gentlemen, I'm ashamed of you.

THE REGENT (*aggressively, turning toward* MELCHIOR): Another innocent!

BALTHAZAR: Exactly. A lamb.

MELCHIOR: I forbid you to call me a lamb. I'm a Professor.

BALTHAZAR: An academic lamb.

THE REGENT: It was his idea.

MELCHIOR: My intentions were of the best. The plan was flawless, strictly scientific. Without that deplorable accident, that gust of wind . . .

GASPAR (*still in his corner, turns toward the others*): Accident? It wasn't an accident!

MELCHIOR: Not an accident? Who could have foreseen that it would blow him away?

GASPAR: We could have. (*He approaches the group.*) We should have foreseen it. (*He holds out the two heads.*) Look at these heads. Twins. More than twins! As if one man had been his own brother. Could we really believe that the paths of their lives, united forever, would suddenly part?

THE REGENT: I'm beginning to understand.

GASPAR: We trifled with the providence that joined them in their mothers' wombs. Or even before, at the beginning of Creation. No, still earlier. In God's idea of the Creation, in the idea of the idea, the presentiment of the presentiment . . .

MELCHIOR: But that gust of wind . . .

GASPAR: The gust of wind is unimportant. A mere tool in the hand of providence. Their fates were identical. When one perished, the other had to perish.

MELCHIOR: Then it's all the fault of destiny.

GASPAR: Oh no! We are to blame for not having suspected so simple a consequence. We took the first step, destiny merely completed our work because it had to obey its own laws. We, the Three Wise Men from the East! Some wise men we turned out to be!

THE REGENT: Isn't that lovely? I suspected this mess was your doing.

BALTHAZAR (*trying to make light of the matter, speaking of* GASPAR): He's feverish.

MELCHIOR: You're not going to listen to the ravings of a madman?

GASPAR: What blindness! It should have been obvious that their destinies were inseparable! Oh folly of the wise!

MELCHIOR *and* BALTHAZAR *fling themselves on* GASPAR *and put their hands over his mouth.*

MELCHIOR: He shouldn't talk so much. It tires him.

BALTHAZAR: He needs rest.

THE REGENT: He's said enough. Now we know who'll have to answer for all this.

MELCHIOR AND BALTHAZAR (*in unison*): Answer? To whom?

THE REGENT: To the infuriated people. (*Lightning, thunder, and the roaring of the crowd in crescendo:* "The Pro-phet, the Pro-phet!" THE REGENT *raises his hand and holds out his forefinger.*) Do you hear that? The storm!

Loud rhythmic roaring of the crowd. Slow, measured drum beats, that is, the blows of a battering ram against the palace doors.

THE BAILIFF (*on the balcony, looking over the square*):
They're smashing the door in!

THE REGENT: Their patience is at an end.

MELCHIOR (*still gagging* GASPAR *with the help of* BAL-
THAZAR): Regent, do something. Save us!

THE REGENT: My role is ended. There's nothing I can do.

BALTHAZAR: Maybe we could wait. There have been two,
maybe there will be a third.

MELCHIOR: Preposterous! How often does a Prophet turn
up? Once every five hundred, seven hundred years.
This is a matter of minutes.

THE BAILIFF (*from the balcony*): The door won't hold,
boss.

THE REGENT: Go down and open it. Tell them to come in.
Tell them I'll explain everything. The guilty parties
will answer to the people's court.

THE BAILIFF: I should let them into the palace?

THE REGENT: I have spoken. Hurry! (*To* MELCHIOR *and*
BALTHAZAR.) I trust that Professor Gaspar will repeat
his deposition in court.

THE BAILIFF: They're going to mess up my floors. (*He moves
reluctantly to stage left.*)

MELCHIOR (*to* THE BAILIFF): Stop! (*To* THE REGENT.)
You're going to hand us over?

THE REGENT: I'm going to deliver you to the judgment of
disappointed humanity.

MELCHIOR: To the lynch justice of the mob. You think you
can save your skin at our expense.

THE REGENT: The people will judge.

MELCHIOR (*to* BALTHAZAR): Seize him!

MELCHIOR *and* BALTHAZAR *abandon* GASPAR *and rush at* THE REGENT. THE REGENT *runs around* GASPAR, *who stands motionless.*

THE REGENT (*running*): Bailiff! Help!
THE BAILIFF: Coming, boss.

He joins the others and all run after THE REGENT *around* GASPAR, *who is standing motionless in the center of the stage.*

THE REGENT: Faster!
THE BAILIFF: I can't, boss. You're too quick for me.
THE REGENT: Idiot! Why are you chasing me?
THE BAILIFF: You told me to run.
GASPAR (*raising high the heads*): Your hour has struck! (*The crowd chants rhythmically:* "The Pro-phet . . . the Pro-phet.") He's coming! He has come! (*He goes toward the balcony.*)
MELCHIOR (*stops running*): What's he going to do . . . ?
BALTHAZAR (*also stops*): Something idiotic. It won't be the first time. He makes the bed and we have to . . .

GASPAR *goes out on the balcony.*

MELCHIOR: Stop him!

MELCHIOR *and* BALTHAZAR *rush out on the balcony.* THE BAILIFF *stops running after* THE REGENT *and goes off to one side. Taking advantage of the diversion,* THE REGENT *heads stage right on tiptoes. As he nears the door, he breaks into a run and vanishes.*

GASPAR (*on the balcony, arms lowered so the people cannot see the heads of the Prophets*): People, give ear!

The cries and the drum stop. Total silence.

BALTHAZAR: Too late.

> MELCHIOR *and* BALTHAZAR *station themselves on either side of the door to the balcony and look cautiously out.*

GASPAR: Here is your Prophet! (*He raises one arm and shows the people one of the heads. A moment's silence, then a great outburst of laughter on the square.*) What? Not this one? I must have made a mistake... (*He lowers his arm and raises the other head. The laughter increases. Disconcerted,* GASPAR *raises first one arm, then the other, like a sailor wigwagging. From the square Homeric laughter.* GASPAR *raises both heads at once. A still louder burst of laughter, mingled with catcalls.* GASPAR *bows his own head and slowly leaves the balcony.*) Why are they laughing?

THE BAILIFF: They're always like that. Haven't you ever heard them at the movies?

GASPAR (*holding out the two heads*): What's the joke?

THE BAILIFF: Wait. I'll take a look.

> *He approaches and examines the two heads attentively. He smiles discreetly, putting his hand over his mouth.*

GASPAR: Well?

THE BAILIFF (*tittering*): They're... sort of ... chopped off.

> *Cries of rage from the crowd.*

MELCHIOR (*to* GASPAR): Now you've done it! Now they know we've liquidated all the Prophets!

GASPAR: They would have crucified them anyway!

MELCHIOR: That's exactly why they'll never forgive us.

THE BAILIFF: They just want to do everything themselves. I once knew a fellow who wouldn't eat anything anybody else had cooked. He hated restaurants.

The drum beats resume at a faster pace.

MELCHIOR (*looking around*): But where's our Regent?

THE BAILIFF: The boss has stepped out.

MELCHIOR: Which door?

THE BAILIFF (*takes the little ball of silver paper out of his pocket, puts it in his right hand, closes his hand and raises his fist*): Eeny, meeny, guess!

MELCHIOR: Stop fooling around.

THE BAILIFF (*opening his hand and showing the ball*): Right.

MELCHIOR (*to* BALTHAZAR): Follow me.

BALTHAZAR (*referring to* GASPAR): What about him?

MELCHIOR: He won't run away.

MELCHIOR *and* BALTHAZAR *run out stage right. On the run* BALTHAZAR *picks up the ax which* THE BAILIFF *had left in a corner, slips it under his robe, looks discreetly around to make sure no one has seen him, and runs after* MELCHIOR. GASPAR *stands motionless, a head in each hand.* THE BAILIFF *goes out to the right and returns, walking backward, dragging a heavy bench of dark, almost black, oak. He puts the bench down in*

*the middle of the stage, parallel to the footlights. He
approaches* GASPAR.

THE BAILIFF: Beg your pardon. (*He takes the two heads and
puts them down on the bench facing the audience,
attentive to the symmetry. To* GASPAR, *hesitantly.*) You
don't happen to remember which was the first?
GASPAR: It doesn't matter.
THE BAILIFF: There's got to be order.

*He reflects, then reverses the heads. The cries of the
crowd have stopped, but the drum beats continue. A
door slams somewhere within the palace, to the left.*
THE BAILIFF *and* GASPAR *turn their faces in that direction.*

GASPAR: What was that?
THE BAILIFF: Another gust of wind.
GASPAR: I'll be leaving.
THE BAILIFF: Which way?
GASPAR: Left.
THE BAILIFF: I wouldn't advise it. There'll be people.
GASPAR: That's all right. I'll tell them everything. I'll con-
fess my guilt, I hope they'll understand.
THE BAILIFF: Whatever you say. (GASPAR *moves stage left.*
THE BAILIFF *pushes both heads further left. He takes
out a handkerchief and dusts the bench.*) What
should I say if somebody asks?
GASPAR: The truth! The whole truth! (*Exit stage left.*)
THE BAILIFF: Some wise man! (MELCHIOR *and* BALTHAZAR
appear in the doorway on the left and step on the

threshold with an embarrassed look.) Did you find him? (*Silence.*) What's the matter? Not giving audiences today?

MELCHIOR: He ran up the stairs . . .

BALTHAZAR: No, down.

MELCHIOR: Up.

BALTHAZAR: Maybe so, I was looking the other way.

MELCHIOR (*ironically*): Oh, you were looking the other way?

THE BAILIFF: Who cares? And then?

MELCHIOR: The Professor here followed him . . .

BALTHAZAR: I beg your pardon, it was you, Professor . . .

MELCHIOR: Down.

BALTHAZAR: Up.

THE BAILIFF: Come to the point. What happened?

MELCHIOR: He slipped . . .

THE BAILIFF: On his head?

MELCHIOR: No, on his feet.

THE BAILIFF: Oh, I thought . . .

MELCHIOR: But just then a barber came by . . .

THE BAILIFF: Who?

MELCHIOR: A barber. I imagine he'd lost his way.

THE BAILIFF: Okay, a barber. And then?

MELCHIOR: He was holding an open razor . . . (*Anticipating a question from* THE BAILIFF.) He was probably on his way to shave somebody.

THE BAILIFF: Sure. Why not?

MELCHIOR: By an unfortunate coincidence the barber was passing by just as the Regent slipped. The Regent fell on the open razor and cut off his head.

BALTHAZAR: May his memory be honored!

THE BAILIFF (*holding out his hand*): Let's see. (BALTHAZAR *opens his robes and gives* THE BAILIFF *the head of* THE REGENT. *The head must not look realistic but should be slightly stylized or simplified.* THE BAILIFF *goes to one side carrying* THE REGENT's *head.*) Poor boss! When I think of all the stupid orders I've heard from this mouth ... Go get it, take it away ... do this, do that. Never a minute's rest. And now I'd welcome the stupidest orders in the world if only the boss were alive again. What good is a bailiff without a boss? (*He puts* THE REGENT's *head on the bench beside the two others. He takes a few steps back to judge the effect.*) Actually he looks better this way. He was bowlegged. (*To the two* WISE MEN.) You have wronged me.

The sound of the drum stops. Excited cries are heard mingled with the barking of dogs as at a hunt.

BALTHAZAR: What's that?

THE BAILIFF: Oh, I almost forgot. Professor Gaspar left a message. He went down to see the people. Something he wanted to tell them.

BALTHAZAR: Tell them? What?

THE BAILIFF: I'm not quite sure.

BALTHAZAR (*approaching* THE BAILIFF *threateningly*): If I were you, I'd try to remember.

THE BAILIFF (*quickly*): Some truth, I think.

MELCHIOR AND BALTHAZAR (*in unison*): What truth?

THE BAILIFF: I don't know.

MELCHIOR *and* BALTHAZAR *rush at him and seize him by the lapels.*

MELCHIOR: Speak!

THE BAILIFF (*frightened*): The truth! The whole truth!

MELCHIOR (*letting* THE BAILIFF *go; to* BALTHAZAR): Quick! Quick!

The two WISE MEN *rush off to the right,* THE BAILIFF *looks after them. The cries and the barking of the dogs die down gradually.*

THE BAILIFF: What a hurry they're in! They must want to hear it too . . . (*Pause.* THE BAILIFF *paces the floor.*) Sure. Everybody wants to know the truth. (*He stops, facing the audience.*) Can't they get along without it? (*He goes out to the left and comes back dragging a chair. In his left hand he holds a saucer and a cup of tea. In the cup, a spoon. He puts the saucer on the end of the bench, leaving a space between the cup and the heads. He puts the chair down beside the bench and sits down, turning his profile to the audience. He takes off his helmet, pushes it under the chair, stirs his tea with a tinkling sound. Backstage the sounds of the dogs and hunters resume.* THE BAILIFF *turns his face toward the balcony.*) Hey! Hey! Time to knock off for lunch! Regulations! (*The tumult continues.*) Can't they see I need a rest? Oh well, a job is a job! (*He rises with an effort, goes out on the balcony and leans over the rail.*) Okay, toss it up! (*The tumult dies down.* BALTHAZAR's *head flies into the air, thrown like a ball.*) That's the stuff! (THE BAILIFF *catches it in midair, comes back into the hall, and sets it down beside* THE REGENT's *head. He returns to the balcony.*) Hey! Can't you aim a little better? (MELCHIOR's *head flies up.*) That's it! (THE BAILIFF *catches it and cries out affably.*) Many thanks! (*He returns to the hall.*) Oh, the stinkers! They've bumped off the whole delegation. If a Prophet turns up now, who's going to welcome him? I wouldn't know how, it takes education. (*He puts* MELCHIOR's *head beside* BALTHAZAR's *and counts the heads.*) One, two, three, four . . . Four victims, not counting the lion . . . Five . . . Say, what's this? Something's wrong. (*He counts again in an undertone, pointing his finger at each head in turn.*) There's one missing. (*Enter* GASPAR *carrying his own head, which he hands to* THE BAILIFF. THE BAILIFF, *severely.*) You're lucky I'm in a good humor. We don't go in for jokes around here. This is a place of business. (*The headless* GASPAR *bows and goes out.* THE BAILIFF *puts his head beside* MELCHIOR's. *Now all the heads are carefully lined up on the bench. The cup of tea is included in the symmetry.*) At last we've got some order. Did you say something, boss? (*Pause.*) No, I only imagined . . . (*He sits down on a chair. The light dims. Lightning, thunder, pelting rain, the elements unleashed.* THE BAILIFF *stirs his tea.*) This must be the end of the world. (*The thunder recedes, but frequent flashes of lightning continue to cast a glaring light into the dark hall. The monotonous sound of the rain. With a ceremonious gesture* THE BAILIFF *takes the*